SOME WINTER'S EVENING

ERIN LANGSTON

PRAISE FOR FOREVER YOUR ROGUE

One of the most utterly gorgeous character transformations historical romance has offered up in some time.

— THE NEW YORK TIMES BOOK REVIEW

Wonderfully constructed from start to finish, with high notes of grace and humor, Langston has written a novel that romance fans will treasure.

— LIBRARY JOURNAL, STARRED REVIEW

Smart, sexy, and powerfully grounded in history, written in clean, clear prose-this book is the definition of a Desert Island Keeper.

— ALL ABOUT ROMANCE

A simmering, swoonworthy story that takes you to places both excitingly new and reassuringly familiar.

— PASTE MAGAZINE

Sweet, sizzling with breathtaking chemistry, and so superbly written that the book will stay with you long after you've closed it.

— MARVELOUS GEEKS MEDIA

For all the dreamers—
May you plant those seeds you've been holding.

Every last one of them.

PROLOGUE
OCTOBER 1821

OF ALL THE many creatures God placed on earth to abandon Emilia Davis, little Robert Granger's toad would not, under any circumstances, be the one to best her.

"Miss Davis?"

"Shh." She brought a warning finger to her lips.

Dawes pointedly coughed over her shoulder, an unfortunate reminder he was bearing witness to her unnatural crouch. She ignored both the glowering footman and the burning cramp in her legs to focus on the tall brown grass rustling by the stream bisecting the Granger's property.

"I've almost got him…" she muttered under her breath.

"Miss Davis, if you please. Mrs. Granger would like a word."

Emilia did *not* please. She very much regretted being summoned by judgmental Mrs. Granger in her present condition. She was vaguely aware of her muddy skirts but acutely aware of her nose, chapped red in the late October wind.

In truth, she wasn't enjoying herself at the moment. But she'd promised Robbie a toad.

"Miss Davis—"

"Thank you, Dawes." Emilia worked to keep her tone patient.

The servants barely tolerated her, as it were; it wouldn't do to be rude.

A small flash of brown skidded across her field of vision, the weeds whispering tetchily at the intrusion. *There you are.* She peered closely at the muddy, tangled roots.

Two black eyes stared squatly back at her.

The toad and Emilia moved at the same time—two sideways lunges, one far more graceful than the other. She nearly toppled into the icy stream, but her hands made purchase. She slanted her palms over the slippery pebbles, carefully scooping up a tiny, leathery-skinned rascal.

"Got you," she whispered triumphantly.

She rose to her feet, cupping the toad in her hands, and her cramped legs sang with relief. "Dawes, would you please hand over that jar? It's on the large rock, just behind you."

His lip curling in distaste, Dawes begrudgingly gave her the jar. Emilia gently nestled the toad inside, on top of some previously arranged grass and leaves, before tying a cheesecloth across the top.

"There now. All safe and snug," she reassured the toad. "You'll be back in your cozy burrow by tomorrow evening. I'll be sure no harm befalls you in the meantime, little friend."

Dawes frowned.

"Thank you for indulging my tête-à-tête." Emilia smiled at the standoffish footman. "Or should I say *toad*-a-tête?"

She laughed at her own joke; Dawes did not. This was unsurprising. Emilia had been Robert Granger's governess for eighteen months, and in that time, she'd made absolutely no headway ingratiating herself with the household servants.

"It's for Robbie's lesson." She attempted an explanation even though the footman hadn't asked. "We're studying the natural world. Robbie will make a little habitat, and he can—"

"Mrs. Granger is waiting in the parlor." Dawes turned on his heel and started back toward the house. "If I were you, I'd leave the toad."

MRS. GRANGER's parlor was done up in green, and there was nothing tasteful about it. The room was garishly green; it was egregiously green. The matching velvet sofas were the color of grass, the drapes deep emerald, the wallpaper striped lime. The parlor was objectively ghastly in a way Emilia appreciated. It served as a reminder that Mrs. Granger was human.

Emilia clung to that reminder now, as tightly as she clung to the jar with her captured toad.

"I...I don't understand." Her mouth fumbled the lie, because of course she understood. She was clever and observant—two attributes which had allowed her to rise to her station and ensured she always understood exactly what that station entailed.

"You are relieved of your duties," Mrs. Granger repeated briskly. "We no longer require a governess."

Emilia stared at the sofa, drinking in the vibrant hue, as if the verdant upholstery would deflect Mrs. Granger's words. She coveted those grass-green velvet sofas. They were what she would choose, if she could keep anything from this house.

It was her own odd little game, carried over from childhood, meticulously constructing a doll's house in her mind. A pretend place that was hers alone, filled with the most eclectic, welcoming bits of every place she'd ever lived. Aunt Davis's copper kettle. Harriet's embroidered quilt. The lace doilies covering every side table at the Hudson house, terribly impractical, yet so wonderfully fancy. Emilia thought a hideous green sofa would nicely offset the fanciness.

"Have you..." Emilia cleared her throat. "Have you made alternate arrangements for Robbie's education?" It wasn't her business; she shouldn't ask...except Robbie's education *was* her business.

It was, quite frankly, the *entirety* of her business.

"Robert shall start with a tutor." Mrs. Granger sniffed.

Emilia's stomach sank. It was what she had feared. A tutor was arguably, *asininely*, the more appealing option for a boy of nine. A tutor had a public-school education—Eton or Harrow, perhaps Oxford—and families like the Grangers believed their schoolbooks were gilded, especially compared to Emilia's texts, purchased secondhand and taught to her at a modest boarding school.

"We had an accord," Emilia said slowly. "You said…"

She trailed off, watching Mrs. Granger pour tea she wouldn't invite the governess to drink. Emilia wasn't permitted to enjoy the green sofas. Her interactions in this room had been perfunctory. As, apparently, was her remaining time in the Granger household.

"That is, I had the impression I would remain Robbie's governess until he starts at Eton."

She thought of the boy's sweet, freckled face, always smiling under his shock of red hair. He called her Davey to tease her. Sometimes, he still held her hand when they walked into town. She snuck him extra pudding on Sundays, and he always shared it with her.

With a surge of mortification, she realized she was still holding the toad. Carefully, she set the jar on a console table. The toad huddled behind the grass, and Emilia all at once felt atrocious for removing him from his creek-side sanctuary.

"There's nothing to be done," Mrs. Granger said crisply. "Robert's uncle has already hired a tutor, and he starts this week. I do apologize for the short notice."

Emilia doubted the sincerity of her apology, but in all other regards, Mrs. Granger was right. There was nothing to be done. She was a nursery governess; her role was to manage a child's primary education before they were ready for advanced subjects beyond the breadth of Emilia's expertise. She had known this would happen eventually. It had already happened three times in the last six years.

She was well aware her place in any household was tenuous and temporary.

"I suppose..." Emilia stared at the toad, trying not to think of how excited she'd been about Robbie's lesson. Her fingers skated over her skirt, worrying at a snag in the well-worn wool. "I suppose I'll write to the agency...or place an advertisement...see about securing another situation..."

She considered her leather trunk, purchased with her first three months of pay when she was eighteen years old, and cataloged its meager holdings. Two dark gowns, a passably nice shawl, her mother's replica silver hairpin, which she never wore for fear she'd lose it. Sturdy boots. Her favorite book of poems. A nice set of quills.

It wouldn't take her more than a quarter hour to disappear from the Granger household.

Emilia could fit the entirety of her twenty-four years of life inside that trunk, and she would carry that trunk for her entire life. Her existence was marked by thresholds: always coming...always, *always* going. Her aunt and uncle's home. Her cousin's farm. Miss Prestwick's school. The Balfours. The Hudsons. The Crowes.

And now the Grangers.

Emilia's throat burned. She needed to leave the parlor. She needed to sit on her tiny, narrow bed and have a big, wide cry. Then she'd dry her tears and get on with it.

"Very well." Mrs. Granger rapped her knuckles on the table, drawing Emilia's wavering attention back to her. "That will be all, Miss Davis. I hope you understand."

"I understand, Mrs. Granger." Emilia smiled tightly. "A governess, after all, will have many families."

And not one will belong to her.

She shook off her melancholy and squared her shoulders. This was her lot in life, and it was a far better life than an orphaned waif like her should have. Emilia would keep moving forward with middling grace and ample good humor.

She had no choice. She had long ago learned to be her own best company.

Even so, she would miss the green parlor. It had always cheered her, how it managed to breathe life into a house where it so clearly did not belong.

1

———

DECEMBER 1821

Gavin Sinclair had spent the last two hours balancing paperwork on his knees and studiously ignoring the snow.

He couldn't countenance snow today. Snow would only cause undue strain, which he wanted to avoid, seeing as he was already shouldering a healthy share of earned strain.

Gavin was a reasonable man. His life was much enhanced by his sound, immutable judgment, and he liked to hope a good number of other people's lives were improved by it as well. He applied that logic now. So long as he didn't look through the frosted window of the jostling post chaise, he wouldn't know if the weather was behaving as it ought. It offered plausible deniability; he could carry on with his piles of notes and presume his conveyance would deposit him at his colleague's office in Reading by six o'clock, precisely as arranged.

Much to his sister's dismay, Gavin had agreed to a legal consultation on his way to Aldworth Park for Christmas. Really, he was postponing his arrival to Cora and Nate's country estate by only a day. He couldn't see how this delay would matter, what with his sister so busy. Her latest letter had detailed an alarmingly robust plan for situating her new governess—who else but his sister and brother-in-law would hire a governess the week before Christmas? Cora would just have to be appeased by the fact that Gavin, despite his increasing workload, would be in residence for *most* of the holiday festivities.

Besides, there was nothing to be done. He'd promised Warren he'd help with a petition, and Gavin loathed breaking a promise.

A problem, apparently, Samuel Norwood did not share.

The carriage lurched and upended his papers. He scooped them up, fumbling in his fingerless mittens. At the top of the pile was a gossip rag his clerk saved for him. Gavin himself did not credit gossip rags, but he had to admit they had distinct business advantages. Or, in this case, distinct headaches.

This Christmastide, St. James Square is experiencing a chill that has little to do with winter frost. Rumor has it, Miss Charity Matthews, a governess formerly employed by the prominent Norwood family, is bringing a breach of promise suit against one Samuel Norwood. Did the young man bed her, promise to wed her, then summarily break off the engagement, as Miss Matthews claims? Or, as Mr. Norwood was heard declaring at the opera, was the governess a seductress? It will be for a jury to decide reparations if the case makes it to court...

Gavin sighed, raking one hand through his dark hair. He tried to keep it neatly combed; it had a tendency to curl, a trait that looked quite fetching on his sister Cora and her passel of children, but on Gavin, only looked disheveled. And while he *felt* harried (all the time, on the inside), he earnestly attempted not to look it.

Though this Norwood conundrum was testing his normally placid demeanor.

Against his instincts, he peered out the window, confirming the rapidly swirling snow. Frost painted the lacquer of his post chaise. The trees along the post road looked as if they had been dipped in icing. If Gavin were already at his destination, the vista would be charming.

As it were, this snow was more foreboding than festive.

He sighed and pushed his reading spectacles back into place;

they kept fogging over in the damp cold of the carriage. When he'd departed London two hours ago, the sky was leaden—the streets and buildings and clouds a uniform sheet of pale gray—but there had been nothing particularly threatening about the weather.

Gavin allowed that it might, very possibly, be a *bit* threatening now.

He resumed his tense ruminations, looking over the assembled paperwork. For the third time, he reviewed the letter from Norwood's solicitor, delivered to Gavin's barrister's chambers yesterday afternoon. *If you are interested in taking up defense counsel for Mr. Samuel Norwood, please write directly. The Norwood family will be in Berkshire for Christmas and would like a response by the new year.*

He gritted his jaw, considering all the angles again. Perhaps he'd missed a detail that didn't make the stakes so hellishly high, he was more than halfway into a stomachache.

What did he know?

1. Mr. Samuel Norwood had (theoretically) proposed marriage to Miss Charity Matthews, his sisters' governess.
2. Samuel Norwood had (probably) broken the engagement.
3. Miss Matthews would (assuredly) sue him for breach of promise.
4. Samuel Norwood was (unfortunately) the son of Bartholomew Norwood, Serjeant-at-Law, a renowned figure in the Court of Common Pleas.
5. Bartholomew Norwood was (oh God, it was so bad) prominent among the serjeants currently considering Gavin's promotion to their ranks.
6. And yesterday (shite, damn it, shite), Norwood's solicitor approached Gavin with the opportunity, upon said promotion, to represent Samuel Norwood in this breach of promise suit.

There was no way around it. Newspapers were already frothing at the scandal, and Miss Matthews would either be lambasted or exalted by the press, depending on how the barristers pleaded. The case was sure to be a well-publicized circus. And as such, it heralded bad, bad business for all parties involved.

But what made it all worse was that it *also* heralded good business. For Gavin, specifically.

His chest coiled with nerves. By many standards, he was too young to be appointed to the elite cadre of barristers permitted to practice in the Court of Common Pleas. But Gavin had no distractions—no wife, few friends, even fewer pastimes. He worked, and he worked hard, and his work garnered tremendous attention. Though notoriety as a rule made him uncomfortable, it also had its incentives. He desperately wanted to be called to the coif; such a promotion was the surest route to achieving his goals. Gavin would *finally* be on his way to securing the prestige and influence needed to make a difference, to help people most slighted by the courts.

If he secured Norwood's recommendation.

Damn it. Though Gavin prided himself on his ethics, he was well aware of the role favoritism played in these appointments. The unstated implication was clear as crystal, the path laid bare before him: if Gavin agreed to help Norwood, Norwood would agree to help him.

He pinched the bridge of his nose and morosely stared out the window. The road was hardly visible through the swirling snow. *This won't do.* Sighing in resignation, he thumped on the roof of the post chaise to draw the attention of the postillion. The horses slowed, and Gavin fought with the ice-encrusted door. With a mighty shove, he managed to open it, promptly meeting a wall of white.

"The roads?" His shout was swallowed by the wind.

The postillion hunched over the horses, and Gavin knew the

roads didn't matter. He couldn't in good conscience continue in this weather; the poor lad would freeze to death.

"Passable," the postillion called back doubtfully. "For now. Snow's blowing more than sticking."

"Where is the nearest inn?"

The young man pointed ahead. "We're not far from Maidenhead, sir."

Gavin looked over his shoulder at his piles of paperwork. He would miss his appointment in Reading, but Warren would understand if precarious weather detained Gavin until the morrow. And even if Cora were disappointed by the further delay, she would want him off the road.

"Stop in Maidenhead," Gavin instructed. "We won't travel further this afternoon."

Gavin wrenched the door shut and packed away his notes. He sat for five minutes before getting it all back out.

Blast it.

He needed to get out of his own damned head.

THE BELLE WAS a tidy coaching inn at the end of a winding lane on the outskirts of Maidenhead. It was also, to Gavin's consternation, the site of a local Christmas party. Today was the 17th of December and in his estimation, too early for a holiday celebration. But that didn't seem to stop anyone at the Belle. It wasn't that he objected to Christmas parties per se, but the frivolity and associated preparations meant the guest rooms hadn't yet been turned over, and Gavin had no place to work other than the noisy, crowded common room. Based on the amount of beer being consumed by the innkeeper, he wondered if the rooms would ever be cleaned. He once read of a man who died after sleeping in damp bedsheets at an inn. Suffice to say Gavin took inns very seriously.

One thing that was assuredly not damp was the spirit of the

Belle's many patrons. By late afternoon, the squall outside had eased, and townsfolk and travelers alight with gaiety spilled into the courtyard, merrily warming their hands at a bonfire while warming their insides with bowls of mulled wine.

From where he sat in the corner nearest the kitchen door—he'd deemed this to be the most likely place to inquire whether his room was ready and his bedsheets dry—Gavin could see that the interior of the Belle likewise evoked holiday spirit. A trio of musicians were set up in one corner, an enormous fire blazed in the hearth, and a pair of serving girls passed groaning trays of steaming mince pies while the red-faced innkeeper tapped a cask of beer.

"Last tray of pies for now," the innkeeper's wife shouted over the strum of the fiddle, which was unfortunately beginning "The Twelve Days of Christmas"—in Gavin's mind, the worst carol. "I aim to enjoy myself for a bit."

A collective groan went up, and the woman smacked reaching hands away from her platter.

Gavin had intended to ask only for coffee—he was behind on his notes, having spent the entirety of the journey fretting over the Norwood case—but decided a mince pie and beer wouldn't hurt, especially as pies were a finite resource. He was at a party, after all.

Or at the very least, he was adjacent to a party. Glad tidings and whatnot.

The mince pie was steaming hot, so he set it to the side and pulled his parchment and beverage closer. He was moderately cheered by the beer. Choosing it over coffee was the sort of thing Nate would approve of. Since his brother-in-law's most recent business travel to London, Gavin had tried to take Nate's advice to heart...but it's not as if he'd had much opportunity to socialize.

He frowned. The recollection of the November evening in Nate's club served as a needless reminder that Gavin's penchant for putting work above all else had not gone unnoticed by his family.

"Cora is worried about you," Nate had said cheerfully as he gestured for a waiter to top off their drinks. "She thinks you work too much. I would like to assuage her concern."

Nate raised an eyebrow, and Gavin grimaced. It seemed he was always surrounded by broad-shouldered men raising their eyebrows. Gavin could only lower his. He'd done so, recognizing the outing for the ambush it was. Despite spending the last two years in Berkshire, blissfully distracted by her very tall husband and very adorable children, Cora remained a first-rate worrier. Regrettably, her latest concern was to see Gavin as happily settled as she was. His own missives, largely dedicated to elucidating the many reasons he *simply didn't have time*, had thus far been ignored.

"Go on then, Sinclair." Nate nodded encouragingly. "Regale me with tales of an unencumbered London barrister so I can give my wife the favorable report she desperately wants." He grinned and swirled his whisky. "It would benefit me, personally."

"I don't have time for *regaling*." Gavin shrugged, pointedly ignoring Nate's innuendo. Nate and Cora were insufferable, but he was used to them. "Nor much to tell if I did. It's been an absolute crush with work lately."

Lately. He emphasized the word whenever possible. *Lately* had a transient connotation. *Lately* didn't mean always. *Lately* sounded better than *every minute of my life for the foreseeable future.*

Nate eyed him. "According to court reports, you're a man on the rise. Are ladies beating down your door yet?"

"No, and thank God for that," Gavin muttered, his ears turning pink. Discussing his professional success and corresponding abysmal personal life was an acute form of torture. "My door remains, as ever, tightly closed. I'm afraid I don't have anything to offer aside from poor dinner conversation."

"Come now," Nate cajoled. "You're nine-and-twenty, Sinclair. There are worse ways to spend an evening than in harmless flirtation. Certainly, it would be more entertaining than sitting here with me."

"In my experience, flirtations can be quite harmful," Gavin groused. "To my confidence, specifically."

Nate appraised him, his gray eyes softening with concern, and Gavin was reminded that his brother-in-law was a good man with good intentions.

"You know, Sinclair, conventional wisdom would be to get out of your head and get a woman under you." He shook his head. "But I'd prefer you get out of your head and get a woman *beside* you. You don't need only bedding. You need someone to read the morning papers with you."

Gavin miserably regarded his brandy. Nate was right. He *was* lonely, but he didn't have the first idea how to fix the problem. Not with work constantly looming over his head. The women he met weren't interested in the minutiae of law, and Gavin didn't have much else on offer.

"Just…try," Nate said. "Not for Cora's sake, for your own. You need to loosen up, Sinclair. See who you are when you aren't being yourself."

Nate had chuckled kindly, and Gavin had managed a tight smile of his own.

Now, sitting in the Belle, hunched over his brief, ignoring his dinner, Gavin couldn't help but bristle. It was easy for men like Nate to dole out these sorts of platitudes, as if secreting sweets to a child. But Gavin was a grown man, and he knew better.

Loosen up. Relax. Stop overthinking. Those were sentiments meant for men with broad shoulders and beautiful wives and good whisky and better jokes. They weren't even possibilities for men like Gavin—third sons with reading spectacles and insomnia. Most days, he still felt like a nervous lad, standing on a steep bank above a stream, watching his older brothers leap with abandon into the rushing water. All it had taken was a single look down, and Gavin could see nothing but his own feet, unable to jump.

In truth, Nate was right. It was tempting—*so* tempting—to not be himself for a spell.

"—Name your price, sir." A woman's voice suddenly sounded at Gavin's flank, interrupting his woolgathering.

He blinked, pushing up his spectacles as he dragged his gaze from his notes to a dark skirt. He followed the skirt up as it transformed into a long swathe of gray wool, closely fitted to the curve of a hip, where a slender hand rested, a forefinger tapping. The gray wool bloomed into a bodice, skating over the crests of two shapely breasts, between which rested the knot of a patterned handkerchief. Gavin swallowed. The handkerchief was draped around a delicate collarbone, giving way to a pale column of throat.

And then he was looking at her, properly looking at her.

The young woman was pretty—the longer he looked, the prettier she became. Wide deep-brown eyes, a round cheerful face, thick hair glinting gold in the firelight. There was a pleasant color in her cheeks that wasn't at all fashionable, though Gavin never understood why.

She stared at him expectantly.

"Er…what did you say?"

A furrow appeared between her eyes. "I said *name your price.*"

The hand at her hip slid into the side of her bodice, just below the curves Gavin was sincerely trying not to look at, a feat significantly hampered by her disappearing fingers. He heard the jingle of coin and realized she'd slipped her hand into a pocket.

Then her words landed, and it was Gavin's turn to furrow a brow. *Price?* She *had* said price, hadn't she? Price for *what?*

Gavin felt his face grow pale before his rushing blood rebounded straight to his ears. *Oh God.* Was this woman…was she…a *courtesan?*

For one wild moment, Gavin thought Nate sent her. His brother-in-law's tease rang alarmingly in his ears. *Get out of your head and get a woman under you.* He shook off the mortifying thought. Nate wouldn't. Moreover, it was logistically inconceivable: Gavin wasn't supposed to be in Maidenhead tonight.

The woman parted her lips—full, rosy—and Gavin's blood ran confusingly in a different direction.

A jumble of half-formed thoughts crashed upon him, the most pressing being he wasn't sure he knew how to talk to a courtesan. Unlike his friends at school and his colleagues at Gray's Inn, Gavin had never been to a brothel...except for the one time during his pupillage when his master sent him to handle a contract negotiation for the proprietress of The Friendly Hen. He had managed all right that day. Not only had he ensured the contract was aboveboard, he'd also helped one of the girls balance her accounts.

"Sir?" The possible courtesan was still looking at him.

What...what was happening? Why had she sought *him* out? Did Gavin seem as if he routinely paid for a tumble? Did he seem as if he provided financial advice to working women?

Did he seem so pathetically, so obviously lonely?

"Madam." Gavin cleared his throat; he needed to treat this delicately. "Please don't take this as an insult to your line of work, but I shan't name a price. You see, I'm not personally partial to...to paid companionship."

The woman's mouth snapped shut. Her lovely dark eyes widened before flashing in fury.

Gavin winced; had he not been delicate enough?

She reached for his tankard of beer and upended it over his head.

Apparently not.

2

———

EMILIA COULD NOT in good conscience recommend travel by mail coach during a snow squall the week before Christmas. The entire hellish experience had left her addled.

Why else would she upend a tankard of beer over the head of the most perfectly handsome man she'd ever seen in real life? (In the name of honesty, this assessment didn't include men she'd only seen inside her head, conjured from novels. Nobody could be as handsome as that.)

She fully blamed the mail coach—the hours of jostling, the crowd, the cold, the *stink*. There could be no other explanation for her behavior.

Well. Besides the fact he'd presumed her to be a prostitute.

Even so, she had acted appallingly. Emilia sometimes feared her terrible manners were the result of her motherless upbringing, her mother not having had the opportunity to impress upon Emilia more than a name, which had been taken from her own mother, an Italian opera singer. Emilia hadn't inherited her grand-mother's musical talents; she hadn't inherited her mother's dark hair. And she hadn't inherited proper behavior from anyone, apparently.

From a great distance, Emilia took stock of the situation, laying out what she considered to be the salient points of this dreadful day. She ached from hours of bone-chilling travel. She smelled of onions due to the elderly sisters she'd been squashed against since Abingdon. There were no more mince pies at the Belle, which made her want to cry. And this lovely man had the *audacity* to wear reading spectacles which made her want to…well, Emilia wasn't certain what it made her want to do. Surely something else her mother would not have approved of.

Blast if this day couldn't get worse.

She thought things were finally improving when she disembarked from the mail coach to find the Belle rife with holiday festivity. Emilia had never attended a Christmas party, and it seemed auspicious that her first occurred as she was setting out to begin a new position. A new *life*. Tomorrow, she would arrive at Aldworth Park, the estate in Berkshire where—God willing—she'd work for the Travers family for a very long time.

But her good fortune had not extended to supper. After showing her to a room, the slightly inebriated innkeeper regretfully informed Emilia the kitchen wasn't serving at present, but she might ask another patron if she could have one of their mince pies. "They stockpiled 'em," the innkeeper whispered. "Took more'n they need. But I wager one o' these lads'll spare one for a smile and a coin."

Emilia looked doubtfully about the crowded dining room, sorely aware of how oniony she smelled, and wondered where all these pie-sparing lads might be.

And then she saw him.

A man, alone in the back corner, piles of paper stacked neatly in front of him. His head was bent over his work, his shoulders sloped, and his eyes unblinking behind a pair of spectacles. He didn't seem at all bothered by the noise, and his demeanor—frowning over his parchment and quill—was so wrong, so patently incorrect for the occasion, Emilia felt very nearly charmed.

His tankard of beer appeared untouched. And there, beside him, was an *uneaten* mince pie.

Perhaps luck was on her side, after all.

For a moment, she wavered, studying him. The man was clean-shaven and boyishly handsome but for a cleft in his chin, which gave him an austere edge. Dark hair, aggressively combed. His coat was well-tailored, and the cut gave the impression he wasn't broad but lean in a pleasingly compact way.

Her wandering eyes fell to his hands, and her throat tightened. His hands...well, there was no way around it. His hands were beautiful. Long tapered fingers wrapped around a quill. The same ink stains as hers.

At that moment, his spectacles slipped down his nose to reveal an endearing little crease in his brow. The man hastily pushed them back in place, looking up as he did so. Emilia's pulse skipped, then slowed. His eyes were dark blue, the kind of blue the sky turns as the stars come out, the kind of blue that lasts for mere minutes. Except there, behind his spectacles, where the color stayed.

She approached him. How could she not? Those bespectacled blue eyes spoiled her for any purpose *but* approaching him.

That is, until he insulted her and she promptly soaked him with his own beer.

Now, the man jumped to his feet, dripping, gaping in shock. "What was that for?" he yelped, holding his sopping coat away from his body.

"I..." Emilia covered her mouth. Everyone was looking at her. "I was only asking if I could buy your pie," she said haltingly. *Oh God. Oh no.* Now this man would take her to task, would lambaste her in front of everyone. She felt a preemptive swoop of shame, as if she were once more a girl at Miss Prestwick's school. To this day, she wasn't sure if the rod or the words stung more.

"My *pie*?" The man swiped his wet hair off his forehead. His hair was curling now that it was wet, and he looked wonderfully, unexpectedly roguish.

"Your pie," Emilia reassured him. He seemed to need reassuring.

"My pie…" His mouth opened and closed four times in rapid succession. "That's what you wanted to exchange coin for?" He scrubbed a hand over his face. "Of course. My pie."

"Yes." Emilia untied the handkerchief around her neck and handed it to him. The poor man was dripping all over the floor. Though, given the noise and the crowd, she suspected his wouldn't be the only spilled beer tonight. "I tried to explain I haven't had supper, but I think you were distracted by your papers."

She took a deep breath, ready to apologize and hand over a precious coin so he could launder his coat—

"I'm…I…Oh, hell." His cheeks flushed. "Miss, my *sincerest* apologies. For what I…said." A blush bloomed from his cheeks to his ears. "I offended you, and it wasn't my intention. I didn't mean to insinuate…ah…not that there's anything inherently wrong with it, if you *were*—I've seen the bookkeeping, and it can be quite lucrative, actually…and as long as the woman is—" He broke off, shaking his head. "What I mean to say is…I'm sorry."

It was Emilia's turn to gape. He was apologizing to *her*. People didn't usually consider her feelings. It would have been less surprising if he'd told her he was Father Christmas in disguise.

"It's no matter," she finally managed. "I know you didn't mean anything uncouth. It was a misunderstanding…" Emilia trailed off, distracted. He'd yanked his cravat loose when he leaped from the table, and she could see the taut line of his throat. She gathered herself. "I too am sorry. For *my* misunderstanding."

"Oh, is that what we're calling it?" The man appraised her. "The upending of my beer was purely accidental, then?"

"Assuredly." Emilia smiled. He took off his spectacles and cleaned them with the handkerchief. She kept smiling, unsure whether he could see her better or worse without them. "It must have…slipped."

"*Off* the table, into your hand, and *up* over my head," the man remarked dryly. "Of course. The natural gravitational course of a *slip*."

"I believe it was in Newton's final treatise," Emilia teased. "Quite a startling discovery, after the apple."

To her pride and pleasure, the corner of his mouth ticked up, a glorious little twitch betraying his active resistance to good humor. Emilia couldn't help it. She started laughing, an embarrassingly full-bodied belly laugh. But what else *could* she do? This was a ridiculous day. She was tired; she was hungry. She was…oddly happy to be at the Belle, in a snowstorm, making jokes about physics.

The man startled at the sound of her laughter. Emilia knew she was acting like a loon but found she did not care. Nobody here knew the first thing about her. It was freeing. Never before had she had the latitude to dump beer on a handsome man and then laugh until she cried.

"Right." She straightened and plucked her handkerchief from his hands, then dabbed at her streaming eyes. "I suppose you'll want to go to your quarters to change? I do owe you a beer when you return."

"Ah…I can't." The man frowned. "My room hasn't been prepared yet."

"Oh." Emilia considered the situation. He was soaking wet. Surely, he needed to change into something warm and dry. "You can use my room, I suppose."

"*Your* room is prepared?" He seemed outraged at the prospect. "Did you arrive today?"

"Yes." She smiled, bemused. "Just a bit ago, actually. Would you like to use my lodgings to tidy yourself? It's the least I can do."

"I couldn't possibly. It's inappropriate." His words lacked

conviction as he fiddled with his damp cravat. "Though it might be nice to change my shirt."

Emilia shrugged, gesturing to the rowdy common room. "Nobody here is paying us *any* mind. They're all caught up in their own merrymaking. Besides, it was my idea. Reparations, if you will."

Still the man hesitated, even as he stood in a puddle of beer. He apparently was possessed of a formidable resolve.

"Oh, follow me." Emilia turned toward the narrow staircase. "You're going to catch the death of you and leave all that paper-work unfinished. I won't be held responsible."

The man's jaw tensed, the slightest pinch of muscle in his cheek, but he nodded. He painstakingly stacked his papers, tucked his spectacles into his waistcoat, and then, shouldering the satchel at his feet, followed Emilia up the stairs. She was very aware of the respectful distance between them, how he stayed two stairs behind, how it put his head even with the nape of her neck, which suddenly felt very warm.

"I'm just here." Emilia ushered him inside the room. It was nearly the solstice, the days growing ever shorter, and her room was cast in long purple shadows. She stepped in behind him and shivered. Although the fire from the dining room below muted the worst of the cold, the chill up here was unpleasant. She crossed to the basin, broke a thin layer of ice, and poured clean water for him. "There you are. I imagine you'll want to wash a bit too."

"Do I smell so bad?" He frowned at his shirt.

"Not as bad as me," Emilia said bracingly. "There was a whole onion situation on the mail coach."

He kindly ignored this statement as he rummaged in his satchel for a change of clothing…though *rummage* was perhaps a generous interpretation. Emilia could see each article was folded precisely, everything well-ordered. Somehow, she had the sense he'd packed himself, that no servant or valet had tucked away his cravats and braces.

Nor, she irrationally hoped, had a wife.

Emilia shook off the glaring intrusiveness of this thought and moved back to the threshold, mindful to stay in the doorway as the man bent over the basin and doused himself with water. Droplets ran from his hair, over his nose, down the little cleft in his chin. Emilia blinked slowly as he reached for a towel to dry his face before vigorously scrubbing his hair, which was now curling in earnest.

"Better?" She felt unreasonably faint.

"Nearly." He picked up a clean shirt and nodded to the privacy screen in the corner of the room. "I'll just..." He trailed off awkwardly, his ears once more growing red. "Ah."

"Oh." Emilia blushed too. "You need to change. Of course. I'll...stand in the hall."

He frowned. "It's your room. I shouldn't be in here alone with your things. I can just go behind the screen...that's what it's there for. It's no trouble."

Emilia feared it *might* be trouble. Her thoughts were certainly veering toward troublesome, considering she'd just been wondering if her littlest finger would fit in the cleft of his chin. By nature of her profession, Emilia was a scholar. She had an agile, curious mind. It could hardly be helped.

The dusky window backlit the partition, and Emilia tried very hard not to look at his silhouette as he ducked behind the screen. She considered turning around to prevent herself from seeing things she shouldn't, but the sound of rustling drew her and she couldn't stop herself from watching the shadow of his shoulders and arms as he shucked the wet shirt and reached for the dry one. In the thirty seconds in which he was bare-chested, just out of sight, four feet from her, Emilia's heart performed an impressive leap into her throat before plummeting to somewhere deep in her belly.

Her face was in flames. *My God.*

She should have waited in the corridor. She should have waited downstairs. For heaven's sake, he was a *stranger*. He was right to protest coming up here together. Emilia hadn't eaten since six o'clock this morning; she could hardly be trusted to make sound decisions.

"Do you perhaps have a comb?" The man popped around the screen, perfectly oblivious to the fact that Emilia had ceased to function as a normal member of society. "Only if it's not too much trouble. I left the rest of my luggage in the common room." He looked glum. "It's probably been stolen by now."

Emilia laughed, grateful for the impetus to pull herself together. "I don't think there are so many ruffians about. Just too many renditions of 'The Twelve Days of Christmas.'" She'd only been in the dining room for half an hour, and the fiddler had played through the carol twice.

The man groaned. "It's the worst one."

"So many fowl," Emilia mused as she opened her trunk. "Why so many? It would be a nuisance." She handed him her comb. "Here you are."

He moved to the looking glass and tried to attack his hair into submission. She permitted herself a moment to mourn his damp curls.

"Are you staying in Maidenhead for Christmas?" the man asked, gesturing in the mirror to her large trunk.

Emilia shook her head. "Just tonight. But I *am* moving to a new residence." She rippled with apprehension. She sincerely hoped Aldworth Park would be her new residence. Emilia badly, *badly* needed employment with the Travers family to last.

It had taken her six weeks to secure the position. Six agonizing, nail-biting weeks, and not even her intrepid daydreaming could distract from the fact that her meager savings was dwindling. She'd spent those six weeks penning letter after letter, querying her meager connections, and posting frightfully costly advertisements while she cleaned her boarding house in exchange for meals.

In low moments, it occurred to Emilia that the letter she *should* be writing was to her cousin, but Emilia wouldn't beg kindness from an unkind man. Since her childhood, it had been made painfully, explicitly clear Emilia was a burden—her parents had left her just enough funds to see to her education but not nearly enough for a dowry. And certainly not enough to entice any of her distant relations to care for her in the way a child needs. Her cousin would be polite when he rebuffed her, but he would rebuff her all the same.

Then, just as November drew to a close, just as things were looking quite grim indeed, the tide turned in Emilia's favor. Finally, *finally*, a reply to her most recent advertisement. Mrs. Nathaniel Travers of Aldworth Park was seeking a governess for the primary education of her son Leo, the ninth Viscount Dane.

Emilia had anxiously written to Mrs. Travers, trying to keep a firm hold on her burgeoning hope. To her immense relief, the response was warm and effusive. Through the course of their correspondence—yes, Emilia could start immediately; no, Emilia had no plans for Christmastide; no, Emilia's family wouldn't miss her—Mrs. Travers must have gleaned the truth: Emilia had nowhere else to go. It was an unspeakable kindness when she suggested Emilia come this week to meet the children and settle in. *Please*, Mrs. Travers's final letter said. *Come for Christmas. We would love to meet you.*

"You're moving?" the man asked, still frowning at her trunk. He was likely perplexed as to why she was relocating with so few belongings.

"For work," Emilia confirmed. "I'm starting a new position this week. Finally." She released a soft, nervous laugh. "I'm *finally* starting a new position."

Her vision was distorted by sudden tears; she blinked rapidly, mortified but unable to halt her visceral reaction. It happened every time she thought about the last few dreadful months—the abrupt dismissal from the Granger household; the humiliation of cleaning the boarding house; the despair as her advertisements went unanswered; the looming misery of another lonely Christmas. The fact that Nathaniel and Cora Travers had altered Emilia's course didn't make those hard feelings go away.

This stranger might think her trunk empty, but Emilia knew how much she carried. The weight of her circumstances had been crushing her since she was three years old.

Of course, this man didn't know any of that.

And…

Emilia's heartbeat quickened.

And he didn't need to know.

She stared at him, pierced with a sudden, startling possibility.

He didn't need to know *anything* about her.

If she told this man she was a homeless governess, their fledgling companionship would fade. He would either pity her or keep his distance in an effort to ensure propriety. It was the same, always, everywhere she went. She was preemptively cast into ridiculous boxes—below the family, above the servants, no opportunity to cultivate friendships, to be courted, to be somewhere other than the margins.

Tonight, Emilia didn't want to keep to herself. She wanted to enjoy the party, the carols, the fellowship of this kind man with blue eyes.

It might be the only time she ever could.

"What sort of work—"

Emilia shook her head, abruptly cutting him off. "No."

"Pardon?"

"I do not wish to talk about my work." She closed her trunk with a decisive thud and regarded him. "I don't have much, but I *do* have this unexpected, unconstrained evening. I find myself at a crossroads…something just ended, something about to start." She took a deep breath. "And I don't really care to think about either right now."

He was looking at her with that charming little wrinkle in his brow.

"I realize it seems mad, but I'd rather like to set aside my real life today." She raised her chin. "Be above it for the evening."

To her surprise, the man nodded slowly, his eyes flashing with peculiar recognition. "Get outside of your head," he mused. "See who you are when you aren't being yourself."

Emilia felt a burning rush of wonder. "Yes. *That*. Exactly that."

"It's odd." He rubbed the back of his neck, a lovely pink glow painting his ears. "But I didn't expect to be here tonight. I was meant to be at an appointment. I suppose…I have a free evening as well. I can't quite remember the last time that happened."

"So we're both outside of time." Emilia bit her lip.

"Apparently so."

Muffled shouts and laughter sounded through the window. She glanced outside, looking over the teeming courtyard. In the gathering twilight, lanterns blazed cheerily, illuminating the crowd of bundled-up revelers. Beneath her came the sounds of the fiddle—no longer carols but a country dance.

Emilia wanted to dance. She wanted to dance more than she wanted mince pie.

"Well, that's good luck for us." She cocked an eyebrow, feeling wonderfully daring. "After all, I owe you a beer."

He was silent. She could see the wheels turning, a hundred tiny decisions being weighed and made. He was a man caged by caution.

She decided to open the door.

"I'm Emilia." Surely, her name was one aspect of her life she could share. Especially if it put him at ease. She smiled and offered a hand. "Now we aren't strangers, if that was your worry. Shall we go down to the party?"

"Emilia."

He exhaled slowly, shaking his head, as if wholly unsure of her, of himself. Then…

"Emilia, I'm Gavin."

Gavin.

He took her hand. His palm was dry and warm; he had a callus on his ring finger. The fact that she now knew this unleashed a swoop of heat, tightening her stomach and loosening her chest.

"All right then." He unexpectedly offered a sweet half smile. "Best we don't look down."

3

———

GAVIN'S most urgent problem was no longer the Norwood brief. It wasn't the weather; it wasn't the beer poured over his head. It wasn't even the possibility of an ill-begotten chill from damp bedsheets—thankfully, no longer an active concern, as the proprietor had finally confirmed his room was ready and his bed linens dry.

No. Gavin's most urgent problem was that Emilia had a dimple. One dimple, in her left cheek. This was perhaps more alarming than if she'd had dimples in both cheeks. The lack of symmetry confirmed an impish nature. Gavin hardly knew what to do with polite ladies, let alone impish ones.

Last spring, when he was visiting Aldworth Park, Cora had too much ratafia and waxed poetic about Nate's dimples until Gavin contemplated sawing off his own ears with Leo's toy sword. He could now begrudgingly admit his sister might have had a point. Has anything so directly spelled danger as a dimple? Or were Sinclairs simply more susceptible to them? He tried to picture his elder brothers' wives—did they have dimples?

He first noticed the dimple when she teased him about slipping with his beer. He feigned wiping off his spectacles because he didn't know what else he was meant to do. Since then, he'd tried not to look at it, even going so far as to resist smiling himself, fearing his smile would summon hers, and then he would see the dimple again. It was a damn shame, because he felt he was otherwise doing a surprisingly decent job of conversing with her.

So long as he wasn't inadvertently dazzled, he could go along with her ludicrous plan to attend this Christmas party together.

"Your turn," Gavin said, popping a roasted chestnut into his mouth.

Upon their return to the cacophony of the common room, they discovered the innkeeper's wife and scullery maids had gone back to the kitchens in an apparent surge of holiday goodwill. Platters of mince pies and roasted nuts and gingerbread abounded, much to Emilia's—unfortunately dimpled—delight.

"What about them?" He nodded toward an elderly couple at the end of the bench opposite them, near the fire.

"Hmm..." Emilia contemplated. At her suggestion, they had spent the last hour fabricating stories for their fellow partygoers. "*He* was shipwrecked after finding the lost city of Atlantis. Her brother was his first mate, and he promised him upon his deathbed—oh, I should have mentioned, they were attacked by a kraken—the captain would wed his sister—"

"A kraken?" Gavin interjected. "Truly? You took a point from my last one because I—"

"Said the bald gentleman was a banker."

"And?" Gavin crossed his arms. "He *could* be a banker."

"Precisely. You keep coming up with stories that are entirely plausible." She laughed, and Gavin closed his eyes.

Her laugh was his second problem. It was bubbling and blooming and so unexpectedly robust, it was damn near impossible not to smile in response, what with her being all rosy and dimply and—

Gavin took a long drink of beer.

"Fine," he relented when she finally stopped laughing and

threatening his composure. "I'll give you a point. If nothing else, the misuse of folkloric traditions was inspired."

"So that's..." Emilia tallied their points; she was keeping track with a slate pencil from her trunk. "Eleven for me and one for you."

Gavin's point was a pity point. She gave it to him after a long-winded recounting of the feudal system in an attempt to position the redheaded fiddler as a squire.

"Now then..." Emilia nodded to a knot of dancers. "How about that couple? The light-haired fellow and the girl in the green skirt?"

Gavin considered. He was woefully unimaginative and had less than no talent for gossip. But thinking of gossip gave him an idea. "All right. I've got one." He turned to Emilia, leaning one elbow on the table. "Those two are pretending to be betrothed."

"Oh!" Her brown eyes glowed. "*There* you are. That's a good start! Why are they pretending?" She leaned forward, her face alight with mischief. "Something outrageous."

Gavin lowered his voice conspiratorially. "Custody dispute. She needs to secure rights to her children. Nefarious relatives are trying to take them away, and that man is helping her."

Her mouth dropped open. "And then what?"

"And then..." He shrugged. "They fall in love."

"Gavin, well done!" Emilia tossed a chestnut to him. "You're finally catching onto this game."

She laughed again—that remarkable laugh—and with a hot spike of pride, Gavin was glad he'd caused it, despite the havoc it wreaked upon him. He'd never met anyone so unshackled by good humor. It was unnerving and admirable. Did it always come so easily to her?

It certainly didn't for him.

It defied logic. Under any other possible circumstances—if he knew this woman, if he were in a familiar place, if he were in his normal routine—it would have ended with the beer incident. He would have withdrawn and returned to his work.

Why hadn't he?

A flash of her panicked face right after she dumped the beer, the flinch that spasmed through her when he jumped to his feet. Her first reaction had been shame, and Gavin couldn't bear the thought of causing anyone that sort of distress. So of course, naturally, *he* apologized to *her*. And then it wasn't so hard to let the conversation unwind from there.

Perhaps because she, too, was alone. No overbearing mama making introductions, no cluster of friends watching and whispering. Most of his social interactions in London were laced with expectations. And Gavin had enough of those at work. Everywhere, at every turn, expectations—to do more, to do right.

Expectations were strangling him.

Above it tonight, he reminded himself. *Don't look down.*

But Emilia was looking down, marking his point on the table, drawing his gaze to the nape of her neck. Her hair was pinned up in a heavy knot. It looked very soft. He liked the way it coiled, twisted neatly like a skein of silk. He absently wondered how long her hair was when it was loose, if it brushed her shoulder blades or the small of her back. He wondered how it would feel to wind her hair through his fingers, to feel its golden weight around his wrist.

Bloody hell. He needed to divert these thoughts.

Clearly, the strain from work was bleeding into other parts of his life. Including parts south of his navel.

He looked away from her hair.

For a moment, they fell quiet, eating chestnuts and drinking beer. Gavin briefly wondered if he should say something and tried to think of a topic that wasn't calamitously dull. Then he relaxed; Emilia was wonderfully conversant, which meant he didn't have to be. If she wanted to say something, she would. All evening, her chatty nonchalance had granted him a peculiar, welcome reprieve.

Gavin loathed the pressure of steering a conversation, but he didn't usually mind volleys.

"This is marvelously fun." She looked at him and smiled. "You know, I've never been to a Christmas party before. Everyone is so happy."

"I've been to Christmas parties," Gavin said, watching her watch the crowd. "They aren't always as fun as this one."

"No?" She licked the corner of her lip; the pink of her tongue on the pink of her lip was a firebrand in his stomach.

In an attempt to master himself, he focused on tidying their discarded chestnut shells, sweeping them with his hand into a little pile in the center of their table.

Something was all off-kilter. Their shared anonymity must be the culprit. It felt safe, not having to know someone.

"They aren't always so fun for me, at least," he clarified quietly.

She hesitated, rubbing a forefinger under her full bottom lip. "Am I permitted to ask you a question?"

He half smiled. "Well. Not about our occupations, clearly."

He still wondered what she did for work, why she was changing households right before Christmas, why she seemed so protective of it. He'd been studying her all evening, gleaning details. Her clothing was workman quality, shabby but tailored. She was traveling alone—she'd mentioned the mail coach, which he found worrisome. So she was a servant, possibly…or a lady's maid. Her accent was polished. And she was certainly proficient at dressing her hair.

But she didn't want to talk about work, and for once, he didn't either. Besides, it felt intrusive to ponder too much, to try to piece together what she wanted to keep private.

"Yes, you may ask me a question," he answered.

"Do you have a family?"

Gavin took a drink of beer. "Not one of my own, but the family I grew up with? There were my parents, of course, and my older brothers—I have two. My sister is the youngest and she loathed it.

Four years my junior but always presumed herself the same as me. And I let her. She made it easy to believe she could handle anything on her own."

He frowned at the old, familiar guilt. Though all's well that ends well, he still felt dreadful about Cora's abysmal first marriage. After her louse of a husband died, leaving her in a wretched mess, Gavin tried to help Cora and the children. But he never should have allowed her to pretend to be fine for so many years. In truth, it ate him up if he thought about it for too long.

Emilia smiled wistfully. "I don't have siblings. It must have been rather grand, growing up with them."

"It was fine, I suppose." Gavin considered. "I had a pleasant childhood. Though everyone in my family is louder than I am, so I mostly learned to listen." He locked eyes with her over his beer. "It's not a bad quality, but the trouble is, when you're always listening, sometimes people forget to hear you in return. So this"— he gestured between them—"is quite strange for me." He sighed. "My work requires me to be proficient at orating, and I can do it, but it never feels natural. Frankly, it can be exhausting."

"You're speaking to me," she said lightly, tilting her head.

"Well…you're listening to me."

Gavin's voice fell. Emilia's eyes were burnished in the gleam of the hearth, her lashes thick and dark, which was nonsensical when her hair was so fair. The firelight cast her aglow, except where shadows painted her—beneath her jaw, the hollow of her throat. She was *so* lovely. It made his chest heavy, just from looking.

In a confusing rush, he tried to stop noticing things about her. He instead looked about the lively dining room. Candles were lit against the gathering darkness, tables pushed to the side to create a makeshift dance floor.

Emilia's attention kept flitting to the dancers. The hem of her skirt brushed his trousers, the wool swishing as she wistfully bounced her knee to the strum of the fiddle.

He liked having her skirt touch his leg.

She wanted to dance; Gavin knew this. He'd known it for the last quarter hour. He was trying to get there too.

"Emilia…" He broke off. He could feel his ears turning red, the flush climbing from his neck. He had no way to mask it.

"Do you know," she said softly, "I've once again been terribly rude. I asked you a question but didn't offer you the same opportunity." Her gaze dipped over him, and the invitation hit him square in the chest. "Is there a question you'd like to ask me?"

He gritted his jaw. He was starting to feel a bit heady, a bit unsteady. But she wanted to dance. She'd never been to a Christmas party.

"Would…you care to dance?" He took her hand and put it between both of his, silently thanking her for the encouragement. Her knuckles were chapped, her fingernails neat and rounded.

"Yes." She sighed. "I very much would."

Slowly, he pulled her to her feet. He wasn't a large man, and standing side by side, he was taller than her but not by much; his mouth was even with the bridge of her nose. He considered adding this to the trove of what he knew of her, but decided it was better that he didn't.

The interior of the Belle was hot and crowded, but additional musicians had gathered around the bonfire in the courtyard. The younger folk had moved outside, using the dark and the snow to mask the things young people do.

Gavin had a choice—the fiddle inside or the fiddle out.

Don't look down.

He handed her cloak to her.

She followed him outside.

They joined the revelry in the frigid courtyard, only narrowly avoiding two young men carrying bowls of steaming mulled wine. Emilia shivered and fastened her hooded blue cloak around her shoulders. She looked at Gavin, and the hopeful surge in his stomach was echoed in the honeyed curve of her smile.

Before he could gather himself, before he could weigh his next decision, before he could even recognize he'd left his hat inside, the fiddlers launched into a Scotch reel. A shout went up as couples raced to pair off, and everything suddenly seemed to be moving as fast as the music.

"Here we go—"

There was a brilliant moment when Emilia's hand was on his shoulder, he was touching her, holding her, and then she was spinning away. In a swirl of high spirits, she rotated through the dance, changing hands with the men in their set. She was luminous and laughing, her eyes only on Gavin. His ownership of her gaze in this crowd unlocked a startling new boldness within him.

He couldn't have said for all the money in the world what the other women looked like, but he knew the exact moment a tendril of Emilia's hair came loose; he knew she was rushing her footwork. And he knew it would be three more beats until they were paired again.

His hand on her arm, for a longer moment each time, his fingertips tingling. She missed a step, he found it, squeezing her hip for a blurring half second—"Left foot, Emilia, left again"—and then off, away, around, back. Their shoulders brushed, her color high. Off, away, around, back. They met for the circle, her fingers skimming his wrist. Off, away, around, back.

Every time, he found her. Across the fire, through the snow, over the crowd.

Back to him, her hands in his.

Back to him, her skirts sweeping his boots.

Back to him, her laughter in his ears.

Back, back, back.

"Do you want to rest?" he called as she drew near again; this time, she stayed near.

Their breath clouded in the December air, but Gavin felt no chill. He was thrumming with an unexpected, nearly frenetic frisson.

Once again, he took her hand.

Once again, she followed him.

And then they were in the shadow of the inn, in the narrow passage leading to the stable. How did they get there? He was vaguely aware she'd started giggling, her enormous laugh barely contained as she tried to keep quiet.

"Shh," he murmured. "*Shh*. Emilia, why are you laughing?"

"I'm just thinking…" She bubbled with mirth. "I'm thinking about what story someone at the party might make up for *us* right now. If they were playing our game."

"And?" He was laughing now too.

"They only met tonight," she finally managed to say. "They're perfect strangers."

Strangers. The word rang in his ears, fraught with warning. Somewhere along the way he'd become at ease with her, but now the realization made him uneasy. It was true; they were strangers. He would never see her again. He could not allow himself to get carried away. Gavin wasn't so outside his life as that.

But she was radiant, she was beaming, and *there* was that damned dimple. He looked at it a half moment longer than he should have, and the pause was his undoing. His resolve was now in her possession; she tucked it away in the curve of her cheek.

He put his hand there, his palm cradling her face, his fingers curling into her hair, and she wasn't laughing anymore.

She stared at him. Her mouth was sweet and slack and…

At the last moment, he wondered about her name—*Emilia*. Italian. Was it her real name? It shouldn't matter one way or another, but he found it did. He wanted there to be a kernel of authenticity, something true he could later use to prove to himself this happened.

I met a girl at an inn in the snow. She had golden hair and a golden laugh and her name was Emilia.

And I kissed her.

4

———

It was his blue eyes. They swallowed her. She followed them to the side of the inn. She would have, in that moment, followed them anywhere.

These were dangerous thoughts. Emilia had suspected she might be addled from her day of travel, and these last three hours confirmed it.

But Gavin was looking at her as if she made all the sense in the world, and Emilia suddenly wondered if he was mad as well. Would that rectify her situation? If they were both out of their heads, if they were both out of bounds…surely, it formed a new game altogether?

A dark lock of hair fell over his forehead, and before she could stop herself, she pushed it back. His hair was thick. It still held the impression of the comb, except where it curled, just a little, behind his ear.

She touched him there, and he made a soft sound in his throat.

He leaned forward; his hand flexed at her hip.

"Ah…" He swallowed hard, and in the moonlight, his cheekbones were tinged by a glow that might have been due to nothing more than the exertion of their dance.

But perhaps not. Perhaps it was the same warmth rising fast inside her chest, reflecting from her bright eyes onto his face.

"That is…may I?"

Imperceptibly, she nodded.

He looked sweetly determined as he lifted his hand. The reel swelled behind them, laughter and shouts filling the courtyard, but Emilia felt settled and slow.

She inhaled, imprinting scent to sensation—the crisp snow, trampled to slush beneath her boots; the musky sweat, trickling beneath her collar; the soap and ink on his bare, freezing hand.

His hand against her cheek.

Emilia blinked and his smile was close, and then he was kissing her. She was being kissed. The surprise opened her mouth, or maybe it was his lips, firm and dry, tasting of gingerbread and beer. Her hands were useless at her sides, she didn't know where to put them—she thought to put them on his shoulders, or maybe weave them into his thick, comb-furrowed hair.

She wanted to do this exactly right but didn't have the faintest idea how.

She was still sluggish with indecision when his fingers found hers, twining their cold hands together, and she didn't have to decide which preposterous mistake to make, because the entire situation was preposterous. She was holding hands and kissing a stranger in the moon-dappled snow.

His fingers curled over her knuckles; his thumb tapped the faint beat of the reel on her wrist. Her pulse quickened with the same lively cadence, even as his tongue moved, slow and sweet, against hers.

Her first kiss.

"Forgive me." He puffed a soft laugh as he pulled away from her. His cheeks were shadowed by a flush, all the way to the tips of his ears. "I'm behaving beastly. This is…quite out of character for me."

She tilted her head, her own blush matching his. Could he tell it was her first kiss? Was that why he stopped?

"It doesn't seem out of character." She winced at her own clumsy forwardness. "It was quite…nice."

"Nice?" He nervously rubbed the back of his neck.

She nodded resolutely. "Nice is good."

His dark blue eyes crinkled at the corners, and she squeezed his hand. They were no longer kissing, but their lips moved together, all the way into the same bewildered smile.

"We…should say good night." She absently touched her mouth, then looked up at him. "Before it gets too late."

It was already too late. What was she *thinking*? She was never going to see him again. And yet…

"Yes. We should." His jaw ticked. He stared at her fingers where she lightly rubbed her bottom lip. "We should say good night."

His hand slid beneath her cloak, falling firmly on her waist. A thrill coursed through her, the anticipation so blunt, it bruised her insides.

"Good night," he muttered.

Her fingers wound into his hair, scoring his scalp, seeking to unearth those dark curls.

"Good night," she whispered.

He didn't heave her against the side of the deserted stable, though she wouldn't have minded. Despite the strangled desire in his tone, he moved with precise, nearly methodical control. He grasped her waist, pulling her against him, fusing their hips with magnetic intensity.

He walked her backward. One step. Two.

And then her back was to the wall, his hands sliding to her ribs, holding her steady, pressing her spine into the rough wooden slats.

"I told myself, if there was anyone back here, even so much as a lost sparrow, I wouldn't touch you." His lips brushed hers, their breath a mingled fog. "But…"

"But we're alone," she finished, sighing against the hot press of his mouth. *I'm a lost sparrow*, she thought hazily. *But he doesn't seem to mind.*

He kissed her again, again, *again*. Her lips hurt, her chest hurt. Gradually, torturously, Gavin's mouth grew insistent and insatiable, and his hunger ignited her—the altogether foreign idea that he wanted *more* of her, that there was more of *her* to want, that he wanted her enough to follow when she pulled back, gasping for air, his mouth burning beneath her jaw, down her throat.

Their circumstances, their histories, their last names…none of it mattered. Emilia wanted to cling to this wild, unready, unexpected moment for the rest of her life.

"Gavin…" She crooned something wanting and unintelligible against his mouth.

"Shh," he murmured. "I'm here."

She melted into the kiss, fully absorbed by him. The taste of his beer painted her lips; his wool coat dragged against her cloak. He held his hips away from her, bracing one arm on the stable wall above her, angling his body to kiss her thoroughly but not enough to give her the pressure she craved.

She put her arms around him, tugging his hips to hers, gasping at the shock of his hardness against her stomach.

Gavin groaned, the sound fracturing the frigid air.

And then, as if admonished by his own choked need, he tensed, pulling away from her.

"No." He tersely shook his head. "No, we can't."

"Gavin?"

He dropped his hand from her cloak and stepped back, each extraction a tiny wound.

"I…" she reached for his sleeve, stumbling to find the words to bring him close, to keep him from leaving her. "I would…that is…"

"I said *no*." His voice was rasping and raw. He scrubbed a hand over his face, his expression unreadable in the dark. "*Shite*. It's a bad idea. This…all of this is a bad idea."

Emilia was suddenly exponentially colder than she'd been when they stepped outside, colder even than she'd been on the mail coach.

"It doesn't have to be—"

"We can't just…forget ourselves." He sounded half-strangled. "There could be repercussions. And I can't…"

I can't take risks for you.

She heard the unspoken words, as clearly as if he'd shouted them, and she understood the enchantment was broken.

Gavin didn't want her. Whatever he'd seen in her, he clearly found lacking.

Emilia wasn't a fool. She knew they shouldn't be carried away. But she wasn't ready for the night to end. She wanted to hold on to the sense of sharing something with someone for a little longer. It was so immeasurably rare for her to have this, she would take it under any guise.

"I need to…I need to go," he muttered, stepping toward the courtyard. His hands burrowed into his hair, where her fingers had just been. "I can't do this."

"Gavin—"

She didn't even know his last name.

"Gavin, wait."

He stopped, looked back, and Emilia wilted with the understanding it would be the last she ever saw of him. In the shadowed passage, she could hardly make out his fist opening and closing at his side, the severe set of his jaw. He looked cold and miserable and she abruptly, fervently wished she'd never dumped beer on him. She wished she'd never gotten off the mail coach. She wished—

"Merry Christmas, Emilia."

And then he was gone, disappearing around the corner into the crowded courtyard.

And she was in the snow.

Alone.

WHEN EMILIA AWOKE in the early gray of morning, she was stiff from the hard bed and soft from her bruised feelings. The entirety of the previous night rushed over her in a tangle of warmth and wonder, only to end in cold confusion.

She had been kissed.

She had been dismissed.

It shouldn't sting; she was well-acquainted with this particular ache. How many times in her life had she been turned out, cast aside? She had hugged Robbie Granger goodbye less than two months ago.

But this was different. Perhaps because last night, with Gavin, she hadn't been trying to be anything except herself.

Emilia's eyes grew hot and blurry. She had thought...well, it didn't matter what she'd thought, because she'd been wrong. She certainly hadn't started the evening with any expectations beyond some company for the party. But as she came to know Gavin, she'd allowed herself to hope he was getting to know her too, the real her, just as she was, that he likewise might have been overcome by the remarkable ease between them.

In the courtyard, her heart left her body; it floated away during the reel. She'd never felt so bright as she did during that dance, scarcely aware of the snow dampening her boots and the other men she partnered with, because she felt nothing, *nothing* except the sharp, wondrous heat in Gavin's gaze. He'd carried that heat to the stable, had pressed it over her with the plane of his body.

But then—*poof*, all the warmth was gone...if it had ever really been there at all. Something else for her imaginary dollhouse, the one thing she never, ever permitted herself to put there: a man. A man with curling hair and reading spectacles, who was attentive enough to tidy up chestnuts yet undone enough to kiss her breathless.

Emilia allotted herself a quarter hour to wallow in mortified misery, staring at the stained ceiling as she tried to alter her recollections so they would not pierce quite so painfully. Gavin's dry humor, his sweet resistance to her, the way his spectacles glinted in the firelight. His hand on her hip, tapping to help her keep the steps of the reel.

His mouth on her neck. The taste of beer and snow.

It was real. It had happened. She would keep those parts, and she would leave the end of the night where the night had ended: in the stable. With the horseshit.

Besides, she had a big day ahead of her. She climbed from her bed and crossed to the narrow window. From this vantage, she could see the dark line of the post road snaking out of town. Yesterday's snow hadn't been nearly so deep as the afternoon wind had suggested; the main thoroughfares would be passable today. Which, for Emilia, meant the last leg on the mail coach and then, finally, a carriage the Traverses had arranged to bring her to Aldworth Park.

She moved to the basin and scrubbed her face with icy water. The frigid rinse was invigorating, and Emilia could benefit from a cold dose of reality.

Needs must.

Eventually, everyone looks down.

5

———

Emilia's first impression of Aldworth Park was an intake of breath so sharp, it pinched her ribs. From the carriage, she spied expansive grounds, covered with sugar-spun snow. Nestled into all that soft sparkle was an ivy-laced manse, the windows frosted and glowing from within.

This was no doll's house. This was a fairytale house.

She was greeted graciously by Mr. Coates, an avuncular, gray-haired butler. To her surprise, the entry hall was already resplendent; hawthorn and laurel and holly-studded boughs draped the sleek banister, effusing the hall with the sharp, sweet scent of evergreens. But before Emilia could exchange pleasantries or appreciate the festive ambience, a tremendous commotion sounded from a side passage.

"Bonnet—no!"

A pounding of footsteps, an echoing bark, and then an enormous brindle mastiff bounded into the hall, dragging her lead as she leaped in joyful circles around Mr. Coates and Emilia. At the massive dog's heels were a small boy, a smaller girl, and a panting footman. All of them were dusted with snow and tracked wet footprints across the polished floor.

"Tess!" the boy shouted. "I told you *I* had her!"

"It was my turn!" The little girl's face was scrunched in fury. "She's my dog too. I get a turn. Every other turn is *my* turn, Papa said…Leo, he said it—"

"Not with Bonnet!"

"Point of correction, Lord Dane." The footman huffed, his hands on his knees. "Your father has asked *neither* of you to walk Bonnet. It is, in fact, why I accompanied you."

Lord Dane. And his younger sister.

Emilia looked them over. The boy had round, freckled cheeks and dark curly hair; his sister was as fair and furious as a snow queen. Emilia felt a twinge of nervous anticipation. She'd never been employed outside the gentry, and now she was to be governess to a viscount. But Leo Dane was still a very small viscount. She was cheered by the manner in which he squabbled with his outraged sister. Surely, he liked toads as much as any other six-year-old boy.

"Leo. Tess." A man's voice echoed down the staircase. "Against my best efforts, we apparently have only one rule for Bonnet. Please tell me you haven't broken it."

"We only broke it a *bit*," the little girl—Tess—started. "But, Papa—"

"Tess, quiet." Her brother hushed her. "Papa, listen—"

"I'll pretend what you were both going to say was *We know the rule. No walking Bonnet when it's icy.* Your bones are too precious to break."

Emilia looked up to see a startlingly attractive man descending the staircase. Tall, broad, light brown hair, an easy, open smile. For one moment, she stared at him, unsure how to react in the face of such objective handsomeness. Then she realized she was having no reaction at all. Her entire measure of handsomeness was a scale left in Maidenhead, at the Belle. If he didn't have aggressively combed hair and dark blue eyes and a chin dimple meant for her littlest finger, it seemed she was impervious.

"Mr. Travers." Mr. Coates cleared his throat and nodded to Emilia. "May I present Miss Davis."

"Ah." The man stopped, his smile widening at the sight of Emilia. "Miss Davis. My sincere apologies for this appalling welcome to our home. I would say it won't happen again, but nobody here behaves, and I refuse to start your employment with a lie."

Emilia smiled.

"I'm Mr. Nathaniel Travers." He came down the remaining stairs and bowed. "Somewhere around here is my wife. You'll know her when you see her, but you'll likely hear her first. She is at present riled up about holiday preparations." Mr. Travers shook his head fondly. "Every other household waits until Christmas Eve to decorate, but she won't be deterred."

Mr. Travers beckoned the children forward, placing one large hand on each small head. "Leo, Tess, this is the intrepid Miss Davis. She is to be Leo's governess."

The little girl's blue eyes narrowed, her mouth opening in protest.

"*And* yours, eventually," her father added. "But just Leo first."

Emilia curtseyed to the children. "I'm very pleased to meet you, Lord Dane. I'm looking forward to our time together."

The boy wrinkled his nose. "You may call me Leo, ma'am. Papa and I agreed, I don't have to be a viscount yet."

Emilia's mouth twitched, and she looked up at Mr. Travers, uncertain how to interpret Leo's pronouncement. She was admittedly a bit flummoxed by the nature of their relationship—given their different surnames and the fact that Leo was titled, Emilia understood Mr. Travers *couldn't* be his father. But everyone—from Mrs. Travers's letters to the huffing footman—seemed to indicate otherwise.

Her confusion must have been plain because Mr. Travers grinned. "If the first thing you should know about this household is our collective disorder, the second thing you should know is we collected each other." He ruffled Leo's hair. "I'm only related to my youngest child by blood. But we don't let that concern us, do we?"

Leo nodded amicably, but little Tess remained disgruntled. She seemed to be having a very bad day, what with not walking her dog or having a new governess.

Emilia squatted next to her. "Fear not, Miss Tess. We'll find something to start you on as well, if your parents are agreeable."

"We have a brother too," Leo said with small authority. "But Oliver has only six words. I think he'll be more interesting eventually."

The dog was still bounding about, adding to the general chaos. "And this specimen of disrepute is Stede Bonnet, Gentleman Pirate." Mr. Travers heaved a sigh. "Known colloquially as Bonnet and my worst decision."

"Oh no!" From somewhere down the corridor came a woman's cry of frustration. "I forgot to have Mrs. Edmonds dry the oranges for the garland!"

"I told Mrs. Edmonds to dry the oranges last week," Mr. Travers called cheerfully. "I know my place, love, and it's to stay two steps ahead of you."

At that moment, a lovely, petite woman with dark, wavy hair spilling from her chignon came into the hall. She had a squirming, sandy-haired toddler in one slender arm and an impressive length of burgundy ribbon wound around the other. She looked exactly like the sort of person who would write generous, congenial letters and invite a stranger for Christmas.

"Oh, Miss Davis. You've arrived!" The woman hastily stepped forward, beaming as her husband lifted both the ribbon and the little boy from her arms. "I'm Mrs. Travers. Welcome to our home. We are *so* happy to meet you."

Emilia looked at the family assembled before her. The smallest boy was dismantling his father's cravat. Bonnet the dog was tracking snow everywhere. Everyone was smiling, except Tess, who looked up at Emilia with a frown. "How many words do *you* know?"

Yes. This would do just splendidly.

GAVIN COULD UNEQUIVOCALLY STATE that last evening's ill-conceived efforts at the Belle—to relax, to forget—had failed catastrophically. This was why he didn't act impulsively.

He was no longer merely stressed; he was *dis*tressed. He was in a state of acute and agonizing stress.

"Sinclair? Shall we begin?" Warren, Gavin's former schoolmate at Oxford, paced in front of his desk. Gavin arrived in Reading an hour ago and was supposed to spend the day advising on an important petition before traveling to Aldworth Park tomorrow.

But Gavin was in no fit state to consult on anything.

What in *hell* had he been thinking? He felt sick every time he thought of sweet, enigmatic Emilia. They'd shared the most unlikely, disarming connection…and then he had to go and ruin it by nearly ruining *her*.

Gavin never ruined things. He had, in fact, directed his entire life to *fixing* things.

"Yes, Warren," Gavin muttered. "Fine, yes. Let's review what you have."

"Fortunately, it includes one more precedent, thanks to your work on your sister's guardianship petition." Warren looked relieved, but Gavin's stomach sank. One more precedent was not enough.

He turned to the window, trying to clear his head and stay present, to help where he was needed.

But Gavin couldn't keep his mind on the law. Indeed, his thoughts strayed dangerously to the illicit. How on earth had he let himself be so caught up?

Just because her hair looked soft and her eyelashes were dark and her throat stained rose when she danced and she had that damned dimple, it was no excuse for his behavior. Gavin had been around beautiful women before, but he'd never experienced such a visceral attraction to a woman's temperament. He couldn't remember ever feeling such innate comfort with another person. It had clearly turned him into a deviant.

Was Gavin now…a *rake*? Surely not. Though it now occurred to him that ravishing Emilia against the side of a stable was, perhaps, a rather rakish thing to do. He tried to remember exactly what transpired, but it was all a hot tangle of lips and fogging breath and finding her body pliant and inviting where everything was cold and inhospitable. He recalled wanting to put his freezing hands in her cloak and allowing himself that, how the blessed warmth of her skin, just beyond her bodice, was both relief and torture. In a way, it had nearly been enough—just holding the curves of her body against the roughly hewn wall and looking upon her with an ache in his chest and heat in his blood.

God, *yes*. More than enough.

But then Gavin had thought of the chill in her upstairs room, and he'd lost the thread of self-possession. At the notion of her in that frigid bed, he'd wanted to put his hand not just under her cloak, but under her skirt. Against her thigh. In her hair. He wanted to cover her with his body and his mouth and—

He *loathed* the thought of her alone in that room.

It had taken tremendous restraint to pull away from her, to maintain his honor, to protect hers. Though honor had been cold comfort last night as he lay sleepless in his own room at the Belle.

By dawn, he'd determined to go to her and apologize for the way he'd left things and the liberties he'd taken. He hadn't conducted himself as a gentleman, and Emilia—with her carefully mended skirt and half-empty trunk and kind attention to him— deserved a gentleman. As he fisted his bedsheets, thinking of her and worrying she was cold, the cover of darkness turned him strangely calm. He thought, if he could somehow hang on to his newfound nerve, he might ask for a do-over.

But by the time Gavin deemed it an acceptable hour and forced his fist to rap on her door, she was gone.

It was then he understood the depth of his mistake: it was *permanent*. He never learned her last name. He would never find her again.

From now on, Gavin would be forced to wonder where she was, who was beside her. Was there someone waiting for her right now? Perhaps a man who wasn't such a useless bloody clodpole as to walk away from the force of her smile? Gavin didn't deserve her smile. He hadn't known what to do with it, and fortune never favors the fool.

"What do you think, Sinclair?" Warren said now, pulling Gavin back to the miserable present. "Your honest opinion. Does my client stand a chance?"

Gavin frowned at Warren's notes. "Your custody petition is sound…" He sighed, his insides twisted in knots that had nothing to do with Emilia. "But I don't see how you can win, Warren. Your client's husband is estranged but very much alive."

"*You* won," Warren insisted. "When you petitioned on behalf of your sister. You overturned her deceased husband's will. My word, it was the talk of the courts."

Gavin raked back his hair in frustration. "My sister won her guardianship suit because she had good men and good luck on her side, not because I was able to bend the law in her favor."

And he *would* have. He had tried.

God, how he'd tried.

"I wouldn't be so quick to undermine yourself." Warren crossed his arms. "Word is, if you're made serjeant, you'll be defense counsel for Norwood in that infernal breach of promise suit." He appraised Gavin. "Not your typical brief, Sinclair."

"The rumors should clarify I haven't yet taken the brief." Gavin grimaced. "I don't even know why Norwood *wants* me to advocate."

"You don't?" Warren chuckled. "I wager it's because you're on an unprecedented run of success. How many months since you last lost a trial?"

Gavin worked his jaw. "Four."

"Four months. My God. Of course Norwood wants you."

Gavin ignored this assessment and morosely paged through Warren's custody petition. But no. It was the same poor outcome for the mother. *What a bloody injustice.*

This, right here, was stark confirmation of exactly why Gavin wanted to advance himself. So many people were ill-served by the law, and there was hardly any recourse. *He* wanted to be the recourse.

If he could have more influence…

If he could plead in the higher courts…

If he could one day be appointed justice…

If, if, *if…*

"Let's go through it again, Warren."

Suffice to say Gavin lost a second night of sleep in Reading.

IF EMILIA COULD KEEP anything from Aldworth Park…no, it was impossible to choose. Over her first two days there, she absorbed a hundred details, and every one was exactly right.

The manse was clearly well-lived in, the evidence of a young family scattered at every turn. Books were stacked in precarious piles—fairy tales and fables interspersed with world histories and geographies, the pages indiscriminately creased and worn. Hand-drawn pictures and maps were tacked to the walls of the nursery; Emilia could only guess someone had been reading the children what she sincerely hoped was an abbreviated version of *Le Morte d'Arthur*, seeing as an approximation of the word *Camelot* featured prominently on many of these scraps. The children's boots were never on their feet, and their feet were never still.

Emilia was delighted. All these clues pointed to Leo and Tess being adventurous and imaginative and well-read. In her mind, there were no better qualities for a child to have.

Mrs. Travers had ordered the spare upper rooms to be closed for winter, but on the main floor, Rumford fireplaces and draft screens kept the living spaces wonderfully snug. Wreaths and garland were strung in the parlor and dining room, and the scent of citrus and cinnamon floated through the halls due to the wassail simmering on the hearth. ("I love the smell, but loathe the taste," Mrs. Travers confided.)

Emilia was shown to her upstairs quarters—a cozy four-poster bed and a sage wingback chair next to a crackling fire—and promptly collapsed upon the goose down pillows in delight. It was the loveliest room she'd ever seen. If the Travers ever asked her to leave, the footmen would have to drag her away.

From her bedroom window, she spied a swathe of the grounds —the frozen pond and a snow-shrouded line of trees. She'd like to walk in those woods later. Would the children be permitted to take a sleigh ride? She liked the idea of being bundled up in the cold, knowing there was a snug room to return to. She liked the idea of doing so—the walking and the returning—on the arm of a dark-haired man with a reluctant smile...but that was a dangerous thought, so she tucked it away.

Emilia decided applying herself to learning the ins and outs of Aldworth Park would be a welcome and necessary diversion from the events that had transpired at the Belle. She hadn't intended to keep thinking of blue-eyed Gavin Surname Unknown, but he seemed to have taken permanent residence in her mind. It worried her, how she couldn't seem to shake him. Then again, it had only been two days. Surely with time, the recollection would fade. It was likely nothing more than the newness of discovering him, the intrusive possibilities he'd unlocked, then packed away again. For a man so intent on keeping firm order, he had proven to be a rather devastating distraction.

"Now this is an important trick. Are you paying attention, Miss Davis?"

Emilia shook aside her troubling thoughts and focused on Annie, Tess and little Oliver's nurse. It was midafternoon on her second day, and Annie had kindly offered to give her a tour of the estate's rather complicated layout.

"Yes," Emilia confirmed. "I'm all for important tricks."

"Good," Annie said cheerfully. "So we have the *main* passage to the kitchens, which I showed you earlier, but you'll also want to know about this back staircase. Come along…there we go. See? It leads straight down from the east wing, which is useful when Mrs. Edmonds is making scones because she'll let you sample them, but only if you're quick."

"That is lucky." Emilia nodded appreciatively as they descended the secret scone staircase. "How will I know if scones are being made?"

Annie laughed. "Mr. Travers will disappear into the kitchens. Not that *he* needs to get there early. Mrs. Edmonds reserves a tray for him." Annie rolled her eyes. "Her fondness for him is *insufferable.*"

She burst into conspiratorial laughter, and Emilia gamely joined in. She hadn't laughed conspiratorially since she was a girl with Harriet and Bess at Miss Prestwick's. She'd forgotten how nice it was to have a silly secret.

In the kitchens, they found not scones but Mrs. Travers, who was going over the final details of a dinner menu with Mrs. Edmonds.

"Oh, Miss Davis, I'm glad to see you." Mrs. Travers turned to Emilia.

"Good afternoon, Mrs. Travers." Emilia smiled.

"I neglected to mention—my days are all mixed up because the recent snow altered our plans—but my brother is arriving today to spend Christmastide with us. He was supposed to be here already, but was detained by the weather, and then, naturally, he had to make time for an appointment with a colleague." Mrs. Travers frowned but quickly brightened again. "He'll be here this evening, and we're having a special dinner. I do hope you'll join us."

Emilia stared. "You want me to join you for dinner?"

In her previous households, Emilia had taken her meals alone; the nature of her employment unfortunately lent itself to uncomfortable exclusion. Last evening, she'd kept to herself, feigning exhaustion from her travels to circumvent anyone at Aldworth Park from having to announce she wasn't welcome. Moreover, she had never, in six years, been invited to dine with the family. It simply wasn't done. In fact, the Belle's Christmas celebration had been the first time Emilia had any dinner company in recent memory.

"Of course," Mrs. Travers said matter-of-factly. "I don't know what arrangements you are accustomed to, so my apologies if asking wasn't proper…but we tend not to be around here. I do hope you'll consider the invitation. Mrs. Edmonds is roasting enough goose to feed a small army."

Mrs. Edmonds lifted a ladle. "Enough for a *large* army. I hope Mr. Sinclair comes hungry. And you too, Miss Davis."

Mr. Sinclair. Emilia dutifully slotted this new name into the dozens of others she'd learned since her arrival. She wanted to be sure to get everything exactly right.

"Where is Mr. Sinclair visiting from, Mrs. Travers?"

"London." Mrs. Travers smiled proudly. "He's a barrister. And between us, he's on the cusp of an important appointment. Even *he* admits he's doing well, which means he's doing *exceptionally* well. I'm happy he is able to come for the holidays. He works too hard. I want him to have a nice quiet rest."

Emilia and Annie exchanged a glance. Aldworth Park had many attributes, but *quiet*, it was not.

"Oh hush, you two." Mrs. Travers laughed. "I can see what

you're thinking. Regardless, getting away from his barrister's chambers will be good for him."

"Mind behind you," Mrs. Edmonds called, setting a tray on the table. "Scones, fresh from the oven." She looked severely around the kitchen. "These are for Mr. Travers."

Annie turned to the side to stifle a giggle, and Emilia couldn't help but grin.

What an absolute whirlwind the last few days had been. A toe-curling kiss with a handsome stranger. A secure position in a wonderful household. New faces, new friends, and roast goose.

She could scarcely believe it, but for the first time, Emilia felt certain she would have a lovely holiday.

IT WENT without saying that Gavin expected to have a terrible holiday. When he finally arrived at Aldworth Park, he was cold, cranky, and sore of heart and head. He felt like a failure from top to bottom. He'd left things badly with Emilia, and he hadn't been able to help his colleague.

Hell, he was even past due for dinner.

Why did *everything* have to be such a bloody mess? Gavin couldn't abide messes. Not even the cheerful sight of Cora's home, gleaming proof of the warm welcome awaiting him, could lift his spirits.

"This way, Mr. Sinclair." Coates ushered Gavin down the corridor. "The family is already in the dining room. Mrs. Travers wanted to wait, but the children were growing impatient."

Gavin steeled himself for dinner. There would be questions, many he wouldn't want to answer. But at least Tess and Leo would be noisy. Cora dined *en famille,* almost always with the children, so Gavin was counting on his niece and nephews to serve up distraction.

"Thank you, Coates." Gavin dug up a smile. "I'm sure dinner will be splendid."

Gavin had to admit the aroma of roast goose was slightly improving his mood. He determined he would eat a hearty meal, take a hot bath, and attempt to sleep for the first time in two days… so long as his mind stayed clear of damned briefs and dark eyes.

Hell. He shouldn't have thought of her eyes. He was abruptly seized by a memory—her bright, glazed gaze, her lips stained pink from his kiss, her contagious laughter as she reminded him they were strangers…

"Very well, Mr. Sinclair," Coates said as they approached the dining room. "You'll be at the end, next to Miss Davis."

"Miss Davis?" Gavin frowned in puzzlement. "I didn't know Cora had guests."

"Miss Davis is the new governess," Coates explained. "She's just arrived this week. She, too, was delayed by the snow. Had to stay the night in Maidenhead."

Gavin experienced a strange premonition. Emilia's hopeful pronouncement rang in his ears. *I'm starting a new position.*

"Miss Davis, you say?" Gavin stopped short, staring at Coates. "She stayed in Maidenhead, the night of the squall?"

A sudden vision came to him. *Emilia's trunk.* He hadn't given it any thought until now…she'd had a slate pencil in her trunk, used to mark points in their game.

Why would a servant or lady's maid have a slate pencil?

Coates was looking at him strangely, but before Gavin could gather himself, a laugh floated down the corridor.

"Yes, of course I can help you cut your goose, Miss Tess, if you'd like."

Gavin froze two steps from the threshold. He felt hot and cold and eager and confused all at once.

That laugh. He was clearly overtired and hallucinating.

Because that laugh was dreadfully, fantastically familiar.

Slowly, slowly, he stepped into the candlelit dining room.

Impossible.

She was *here.*

She was sitting at Cora's dinner table, cutting Tess's portion.

She was looking at Gavin in beautiful, breathtaking surprise.

"You," he managed over the roaring in his ears. "My God. It's you."

6

———————

Emilia couldn't move. She couldn't think. She couldn't breathe.

"You," he whispered, as if he were astonished, as if he had never been astonished before. "My God. It's you."

Her cheeks felt hot and tight. She looked around the soft glow of the dining room, as if the "you" in question were Mr. Travers, or perhaps Marlow, the round-faced footman.

But he was staring at *her*. A small divot burrowed between his dark blue eyes. His mouth opened. Closed. Opened again. He looked exactly as he had when she dumped his beer over him, only more fervent and less wet.

She sat frozen in her chair, clutching her napkin. The clamor of the table dulled around her. She could feel Tess's hand tugging her skirt. She could taste the black currant of the claret, heavy on her tongue. Leo slid from his seat and ran to the man standing in the threshold, and Emilia could now see how similar their features were.

Leo's uncle. Mrs. Travers's brother. The earnest man who abandoned her outside the Belle.

Gavin Sinclair. That was his name. *Gavin Sinclair.*

He was here.

"I…" She had no idea how to finish that sentence. "That is…"

"Miss Davis?" Mrs. Travers tilted her head, rightfully concerned her new governess was gaping like a fish. "Are you well?"

No. I am the opposite of well.

The man—*Gavin Sinclair*—stepped forward, his expression transforming from disbelief into something vaguely familiar. The same look Robbie Granger had worn when the laundress returned his tattered doll, previously thought lost to the lye. The sort of look a boy wore when he was feeling very, rarely, lucky.

"Yes." She finally spoke, her voice oddly thick. "I'm fine. I just…I need…"

She fumbled an excuse and pushed away from the table, making for the side door of the dining room. She was fairly certain it led to a passage between the kitchens and the servants' staircase. She could hide up there. Annie would most certainly be pleased by this chaotic turn of events.

Her entire chest felt sore, her heart gripped and aggrieved with confusion. If she wasn't very much mistaken, the look on Gavin Sinclair's face had been *gratitude.*

But that couldn't be.

Never in her life had Emilia been the person someone was looking for.

She didn't even have time to wrestle with which of those painful thoughts was most pathetic before an arm blocked her progress down the hallway, firmly grasping her elbow and pulling her through an open door. Emilia could hardly muffle a shriek of surprise.

"*Shh,*" a man's voice unhelpfully issued reassurance. "It's only me."

Emilia blanched; she hadn't been in the servants' passage at all. In fact, the cheerful blaze in the fireplace illuminated what appeared to be Mr. Travers's study. One thing she would *not* keep from Aldworth Park was its wildly nonsensical layout.

Gavin brought her around to face him. For a feverish heartbeat, they were again face-to-face, which was an altogether treacherous place to be. His dark blue eyes were heavy. She looked away from his riveting gaze, only to be met with the firm line of his lips and the dashing little cleft in his chin.

Any minute now, she was going to do something calamitously ill-advised. Cry, perhaps. She hoped so; she'd rather cry than compulsively touch his chin.

Emilia stepped back, straightening her skirt, studiously looking over his shoulder. Mr. Travers had outfitted his study with an enormous family portrait. Tess's little arms were wound around Bonnet the dog, who was facing the wrong way. The fact that the artist hadn't been instructed to correct it was perhaps Emilia's new favorite aspect of Aldworth Park. Mr. and Mrs. Travers didn't try to make their family look like anything but what it was—people who found each other and held on tight.

Right then and there, Emilia determined the walls of her dream house would be lined with unfashionable family portraits.

"Emilia." He swallowed. "It *is* Emilia? Your real name?"

She sharply regarded Gavin—*Mr. Sinclair*. Oh God, she didn't know what to call him. Clearly, somebody had to take charge of this situation.

"It is my name, but you can't use it." She bit her lip and looked behind her, ensuring the study door was open. "It has to be Miss Davis."

"I know," he murmured. His cheeks were pink. "I know that now. Emilia Davis. Why didn't you tell me you were a governess? My…my *sister's* governess?"

"I obviously didn't know I was about to be your sister's governess." She covered her face with her hands. *How bad was this? How very, very bad?* "We didn't know *anything* about each other! That was…that was the entire point…why we—"

She broke off, her stomach rebelling. She had *kissed* this man. Her *employer's brother*. As if she were some kind of wanton!

She involuntarily touched her mouth, silently conceding she *had* been a bit of a wanton that night. But she had truly thought it was a safe sort of rebellion. Until now. Because if he told Mrs. Travers, if Emilia's reputation was called into question, it would be the end of her time here. Mrs. Travers was kind, but she wasn't stupid. No woman would permit a harlot to educate her children.

No, no, no. She couldn't leave. Not when she was finally, *finally* getting on her feet again.

"Stop," he murmured, his voice low and hoarse. "What we are *not* going to do is panic."

Emilia eyed him dubiously. He looked faintly panicked.

"You can't tell Mrs. Travers," she said urgently. "Please. Please, you can't ever tell anyone."

"I won't." He shook his head, his jaw tight. "I wouldn't do that."

Right. Of course. It would be in his worst possible interest to tell anyone he kissed her. Why would he want to saddle himself with a mad governess if he could avoid doing so? Emilia stared at him, for the first time fully comprehending what Mrs. Travers had told her about him.

"You're…you're a barrister," Emilia whispered. "In London?"

He exhaled slowly. "Yes."

Her head pounded, more pieces falling into place.

"And your family. Your family is—"

"My father was a baron," Gavin confirmed. "My brother holds the title. I'm a third son."

Emilia covered her face again. Could a woman die of mortification? So far, she'd avoided that particular fate, and her unruly heart had put her in plenty of mortifying situations. But this…*this* put her dangerously close to expiration.

Gavin Sinclair came from a respectable family; he worked in a respectable profession. He'd studied the law, stood before a judge and jury, held the fate of men in his beautiful, ink-stained hands.

"I *accosted* you," she said from behind her hands. She had no idea why she was offering him her hysterics, except he seemed staid enough to take them. Emilia could understand why he was, in his sister's words, doing exceptionally well with his work. He probably elicited all manner of confessions, what with the little curl behind his ear and the serious, open look on his face. "I accosted you, smelling of onions, speaking of krakens. I dumped beer over your head. I…acted inappropriately in the stable—"

"No. Wait just a moment," he interrupted. She heard him step closer, and then she felt his warm hands gently encircle her wrists. "Can you look at me, please?"

She let him lower her hands and met his twilight blue stare. She blinked, basking in the uncommon hue. This time of year, the sky would be the color of his eyes in late afternoon.

"I want to apologize," Gavin said, holding her fast in his end-of-day gaze. "I took liberties with you, and I shouldn't have. It's not the way I strive to conduct myself. I don't want you to feel any shame for what transpired."

He was doing it again. Apologizing for *her* insecurities, just as he had when she spilled his beer. It dawned on her that Gavin couldn't stand disorder; he couldn't help explaining it away.

But he had the wrong idea about this.

"You didn't take liberties," Emilia clarified. "I'm not upset about that." She didn't know *what* she was upset about. That he hadn't taken *more* liberties? That he'd been so good, but also so callous, leaving her alone that way?

But she didn't regret the kiss, and she didn't want him to either.

"Rest assured," she said, dropping her gaze to his shoulder. Her face was surely far redder than his had ever been. "I've never before accepted the advances of a gentleman. It is the only time I've done…that." A staggering look came over his face, but Emilia pressed on. "And I'm glad to have shared it with you."

There was a long, heavy pause.

"So…" He cleared his throat, and she chanced a look at him.

His ears were stubbornly pink, but his face was intent. "You aren't upset?"

"No." She licked her lip. "Are you? Upset?"

"No."

"Right." Emilia briefly closed her eyes. "We are in agreement then. We don't regret what passed between us, but it cannot happen again." She shook her head. "It would be...ill-advised. We're both thoroughly back in our real lives. And my real life requires a great deal of discretion."

And a great deal of loneliness.

"Ill-advised." His jaw clicked. "Yes. So what shall we tell Nate and Cora? They'll be confused about what just transpired at dinner."

"We'll just say we met while traveling." Emilia squared her shoulders. "Nothing more."

For a long moment, they looked at each other, and the looking was sublime. He had given her a flawless evening, perfected by its transience. One dance, one kiss. His breath moving over her hair. His hand splayed on her stomach, warming her inside and out.

Emilia blushed, and Gavin saw her do it, and then they were all at once locked in the rosy confines of recollection, back against the stable, the cold air smelling of woodsmoke and promise.

But now her beautiful memory would haunt her, because no longer was it as fantastical as a dream.

It was reality.

He was here, in her life.

She knew his name.

She knew she couldn't have him.

"Put it behind us," Gavin muttered, confirming both her wishes and her fears. He pushed back his hair, tucked away the curl. "Just make it through Christmastide."

"I don't imagine it will be so difficult." Emilia smiled sadly through the lie. "After all, we hardly know each other."

"Uncle Gavin, why are you holding your quill like that?" Leo looked up from his line of pewter toy soldiers to stare in rightful concern for the writing apparatus Gavin was clenching hard enough to snap.

Gavin blinked; he absently noted he had underlined the same sentence twice. It was midmorning, and he and Leo were sequestered in the back corner of the breakfast room, preparing for combat in more ways than one.

"Ah, nothing, Leo. Let's get back to the game," Gavin muttered. The soldiers were defending Sparta, and Gavin was supposed to be drawing up a battle plan. Which, according to Leo, he was doing quite badly.

Leo returned to the Spartans, and Gavin chanced another look across the breakfast room.

The breached gates of Thermopylae would have been safer.

Emilia was in the opposite corner, assisting Cora and a maid with assembling baskets for St. Thomas Day. Emilia had the gall to be in charge of tying the ribbon, which, lamentably, drew his focus to her hands. Gavin was trying not to stare, but she was looping the knots with deft precision, like some sort of nimble-fingered temptress. From here, her fingernails appeared short, but he recalled with dizzying clarity, they were capable of delivering a sensual scratch. The back of his neck tingled with the memory.

Her fingers burrowed in his hair.

A flare of heat as they scored his scalp.

All his blood rushing, heavy and hard and—

Snap.

"Ah...Uncle?" Leo wrinkled his nose in exasperation. "You did it again."

Gavin sighed and swept up the broken halves of the quill. *Put it behind you,* he instructed himself as he peevishly picked up his coffee cup. *Forget it happened.*

But it was no good. Not only had it unequivocally happened, it was *still* happening. Unless he became afflicted of amnesia, there was no possible way forward for him. It had been two days since he arrived at Aldworth Park, and he was at the end of his frayed and useless rope. At every turn, Gavin found Emilia at the opposite end of a noisy room, but he could hear nothing except the forced silence simmering between them.

He didn't want to forget it happened. He wanted to put it directly in front of him. He wanted to walk toward it.

How was she managing?

From the moment they reached an accord in Nate's study, Emilia had engaged in theatrics of Shakespearean proportions, pretending Gavin was nothing more than her employer's brother, a man she'd met once in passing. She had even taken to occasionally mispronouncing his name, for Christ's sake, which Gavin found both charming and infuriating.

But Emilia's tactics, while perhaps over the top, represented the most rational course of action. Gavin could see why her plan made sense for all parties involved.

And yet, Gavin was forging a different plan, all his own.

A plan that so far only consisted of breaking quills in half.

"Heavens, Gavin," Cora called, her hazel-blue eyes wide with concern. "That's the second time this morning. Are you sure you're quite all right?"

"Never better," Gavin croaked. "Just...tense today."

Nate lowered his paper and appraised him. Gavin's ears grew hot under the scrutiny. Nate might prove to be a problem. He was highly intuitive and had a nose for a good escapade. Gavin tried to think how he might explain the situation to his brother-in-law. *It's no matter, I'm just pretending I haven't put my hands inside your governess's cloak. Nothing to see here, carry on.*

It was untenable. Providence had shockingly offered Gavin the do-over he hoped for, only for him to learn it ended there. Emilia wouldn't risk her livelihood. And he couldn't ask her to. After all, she was right; they hardly knew each other. They couldn't toss aside their efforts and obligations on a whim. No longer were they excused by the enchanting reprieve of a snow-covered inn.

But Gavin sensed his typical reticence slowly giving way to the spirit of competition that fueled him through a trial. It was a puzzle to solve, assembling the pieces, laying out the evidence. He wanted to stand her in front of a jury, explain the situation, and have them deliver a unanimous verdict: was it or was it not all in his head?

Look at me, he silently coaxed her.

Emilia did not look at him, so Gavin looked enough for the both of them. Her hair was twisted back, little wisps curling around her temples. She was wearing the same gray wool gown as that night at the Belle. She'd paused her ribbon-tying to eat breakfast, which unleashed a new torture—she had jam on her thumb. Absently, she raised her thumb to her mouth, as if to lick it off— her lips parted—and then, as if she remembered Gavin across the room, she redirected course, reaching for a napkin and dropping her knife with a clatter.

He was at the very least gratified to know *she* knew he was looking. She kept knocking things over and fussing with her skirt and speaking too loudly to Cora, to Nate, to Leo and Tess, and even to little Oliver, which was the lowest of blows, because Oliver was at present fully occupied with opening and closing a drawer in the sideboard.

"Very well. I suppose that will have to do," Cora pronounced, surveying the St. Thomas baskets. "Townsfolk will be arriving soon. I hope these will suit."

Today was the 21st of December, which meant the elderly and widowed would be thomasing. Most households handed out a coin or measure of flour, but true to form, Cora's baskets overflowed with money and grains and candles and an alarming assortment of foodstuffs.

"You know, love, the elderly widows won't actually be able to carry these home," Nate observed from where he sat dutifully ensuring Oliver didn't upend the sideboard. "They're enormous."

"I put my apple in one," Tess said casually. She was sitting on the floor with her doll. "When I finished it."

"What?" Cora whirled around in alarm. "Tess, what did you just say?"

Tess shrugged. "I've already explained."

"Sweet." Nate raised an eyebrow at Tess. "When you say you added an apple, you mean you put an entirely whole, *uneaten* apple in one of your mother's *excruciatingly* planned St. Thomas baskets, don't you?"

"Well…" Tess raised an eyebrow right back. "I did take some bites. Maybe…half."

"Nate." Cora pinched the bridge of her nose as she stared at her beautifully arranged baskets. "A poor widow is going to get our daughter's table scraps as a Christmas present."

"Fear not, love." Nate stood, clapping his hands. "Right. New game, everyone. First one to find Tess's apple gets extra pudding tonight."

Leo and Tess, and even Oliver, who knew nothing except that destruction was needed, scrambled over to start dismantling the baskets.

"Miss Davis," Cora called. "We're going to have to redo all of these. We'll need some fresh holly sprigs. There's some in the vase on the table behind Gavin. If you wouldn't mind?"

Emilia looked over at Gavin. The vase in question was two feet from his left shoulder.

"Er…" She flushed. "Of course, Mrs. Travers."

She gingerly approached him, and Gavin tried not to be offended. After all, they were pretending he hadn't held her against a stable, a feat made easier when she was on the other side of the room.

"Mr. St. Clair?" Emilia asked pointedly. She paused, as if to ensure everyone who was paying attention—so only Gavin—

heard her get his name wrong. "If it's not too much trouble, would you please hand me the vase behind you?"

"I'm happy to." He kept his tone cordial, trying not to react to the light, clean scent of her soap. "The entire vase?"

"Yes, that will be fine." She smiled tightly in the direction of his elbow.

He reached for the vase, then paused. "Are you certain you can handle the *entire* vase? You don't feel you might, say, inadvertently slip and upend the contents over my head?"

Her lips twitched.

He took this as a good omen. It was certainly better than her staring at his elbow.

"Oh, I would only do something so crass if a gentleman truly deserved it," she said lightly, reaching for the proffered vase.

But Gavin didn't let go easily. It was the closest they'd been in the last two days, and he was once again gripped by an unfamiliar sense of boldness. He knew what to say to her.

"You have me breaking quills, you know," he murmured softly, dragging his gaze over her face. "Forgetting you is an expensive habit."

"I…" She wavered, and he felt a twinge of satisfaction.

"Gavin, can you please not dawdle?" Cora called. "This is a bit of an emergency."

Emilia blinked, and *finally*, her eyes met his. In the bright morning light, he could now see what that dusky evening had hidden; her eyes weren't as uniformly dark as he'd thought, but a shade warmer, flecked with russet and amber. The revelation scalded him with regret. He'd been remembering her wrong. Worse still, at this proximity, he could see the faint impression where her dimple would be, if only she would show it to him. Gavin swallowed hard over a rising tide of yearning. He wanted… what? To pull her into his lap, to work his hands into her hair, to press his mouth against the crescent in her cheek until she laughed.

But more than that, he wanted *her* to want it too.

These sorts of thoughts ran contradictory to the task of *putting it behind them*. With herculean effort, Gavin diverted himself by finding a fresh quill and putting on his spectacles. He would not engage in any of the gift basket dramatics, but he could at least complete Leo's battle plan.

"Thank you, Mr. Sinclair." Emilia cleared her throat, sounding distracted. "Ah…much obliged…"

If Gavin were the sort of man who could raise one eyebrow, he would do so now. Instead, he had to lower his spectacles to see her properly.

She was vaguely glassy and thoroughly blushing. He watched the flush paint her throat, her collarbone, the creamy expanse of skin that disappeared beneath the neckline of her bodice—

At that moment, a cheer went up. Nate had found the apple.

"To the victor go the spoils." Nate grinned wickedly, kissing Cora's wrist. "Which to be clear, love, will have *nothing* to do with dessert."

Cora winked and Gavin rolled his eyes. Emilia used the distraction to hastily retreat to the opposite end of the room, bearing the holly as she joined in reassembling the baskets.

If Gavin wasn't very much mistaken, Emilia spent the rest of the morning looking at *him*.

But he resolved not to look up and find out.

He couldn't bear to get another thing wrong.

7

———

WHEN SHE AWOKE on December 23, Emilia determined that forthcoming holiday or no, she needed to start lessons with Leo. So far this week, they'd only done some light reading, seeing as Christmas was fast approaching, but Emilia didn't want to wait until Twelfth Night to start teaching Leo in earnest. It was nonsense to be here without working. She wasn't the Travers's guest, no matter how welcoming they were. She needed to earn her keep.

She also needed to get her mind off Gavin Sinclair.

She had arranged her teaching materials on a little table in the corner of the parlor. Leo was an avid reader and could manage a primer on his own. But more than that, he loved being read to. After the holiday, Emilia would select a text for him, something she could incorporate thematically into other lessons as well.

But it was two days before Christmas, which was both theme and distraction enough. They had already worked on his spelling and were now moving on to arithmetic. Emilia suspected his focus was starting to lag.

"So, Leo, let's see…" Emilia pointed to the illustrated page of

Mirth Without Mischief. "If your true love sent you one partridge, and two turtle doves, how many birds do you have altogether?"

"Three," he said absently, swinging his legs.

"Four colley birds and five golden rings?"

"Ah…" His little legs stilled in fleeting concentration. "Nine."

"That's quite good, Leo." Emilia smiled, impressed.

"I can count to one hundred." Leo shrugged. "And Papa says that means I can count to any number, because the pattern repeats."

Emilia stared at him.

"Right. Well, let's try this one." It seemed this little viscount could use a challenge. She flipped the page. "What if you had eleven ladies dancing and twelve lords a-leaping?"

"You'd have the Wallaces' Christmas Eve party," Mr. Travers said as he strode into the parlor. "Unfortunately."

Leo ignored his father and squinted, tapping his fingers on the table.

Emilia gently covered his small hand. "No counting out. Try to do the sum."

"Two and twenty." He frowned. "No…"

"Use your slate," she urged him, getting an idea. "See if you can work it out. I'll be back in a moment."

Emilia made her way to Annie's secret scone staircase. Mrs. Edmonds had some gingered nuts in the kitchens. Why not give Leo a reward for his efforts? She was, after all, making the boy do sums two days before Christmas. She already had the sense that little Leo Dane was hard on himself.

Just like his uncle.

In the quiet passage, she permitted herself one rationed memory from the inn—Gavin's somber expression as he told her about his childhood. *I learned to listen.* Now that she'd met Leo Dane, with his dark curly hair and earnest frown, she had a rather heartrending image to go with Gavin's words. He must have looked much the same, bent over his schoolbooks. A sweetly quiet child who grew into a sweetly cautious man.

That is, until Gavin had been neither sweet nor cautious. She thrilled as she recalled the reckless press of his mouth. What would it be like, to not have those kisses for only a single evening? What would it be like to laze against a grass-green sofa with the lean expanse of his body held not-so-carefully above her—

A shuddering swoon dropped through her.

Not helpful. These thoughts were not conducive to the business of *forgetting.* She slammed the lid on her daydreams as she descended the staircase. She needn't arrive in the kitchens hot and bothered over something that had happened only once.

The staircase was dim, lit by a single, high window. In the gray light, she could just make out where the passage turned. She rounded the corner—

"*Oh!*"

"Sorry, I'm sorry. I didn't hear anyone!"

Two ink-stained hands fell to her elbows to steady her. Emilia was on the higher step, which put her a scant inch above him. He was staring at her mouth, and then he looked up, into her eyes. The memory from the stable yard—his absorbing expression as he deliberately tilted her face to his—broke over her in a delirious wave.

Of course. Of course this would happen. Of course this would happen thirty seconds after she'd capitulated to fantasies.

"Mr. Sinclair—"

"It's quite all right, my mistake—"

"Let me just—"

They both turned at the same time, trying to let the other pass. He was still holding her elbow, rotating her with him. She stepped down; he stepped up. Her hand somehow landed on his arm, and she discovered a dangerous new phenomenon. Gavin's sleeves were rolled, the starched linen forming a neat, crisp band above his forearms, which were leanly muscled and dusted with dark hair.

She stared at the skin just below the cuff of his sleeves and felt oddly sluggish. It was skin she hadn't seen before. It implied there was more skin yet to see.

For far, far too long, they stood frozen in the encircling silence, his palm cradling her elbow, her fingers twisting into his shirtsleeve.

"I need to get Leo…his treat." Emilia swallowed, grasping for her wits before she lost them entirely. "If he can add the leaping lords to the dancing ladies…"

"Well." Gavin gave her his wry half smile. "In my experience, that's no easy feat."

But it could be.

It could be easy. No lord, no lady. Just a barrister and a governess, two people who worked hard and kept to themselves. But Emilia could see how easy it would be to keep *him*. She could see it in the way he spoke quietly to her, in the single-minded focus he applied to all tasks, even to Leo's Sparta map.

She could see it in the way he put her at the very center of his gaze, even when she asked to be put to the side.

The safest course for Emilia, always, was to never think about her future. The next position, the next household? Yes. That was a necessity. But inevitably, she would age out of her employment. One day, she would have nowhere to go to except a spinster's house…and that was only if she was lucky enough to save for it. Her future was bleak and lonely and horrendously frightening, which is why she constructed her silly pretend house in its stead.

And then, one day, there was Gavin Sinclair and his reading spectacles.

"Miss Davis?" He was watching her closely, and she belatedly grasped that he made a little joke about the sums.

"Leo missed it by one." She smiled slowly, belying her crashing nerves. "He added them up to twenty-two."

"Ah." Gavin sighed in something like resignation. He lightly stroked her arm, his fingers trailing to her wrist. She shivered and closed her eyes. But he dropped her hand and stepped away. "So damn close."

"A LETTER FOR YOU, MR. SINCLAIR," Coates announced. The butler's shadow fell over Gavin's one-sided chess game. "Delivered a moment ago."

"A letter?" Cora turned from where she curled near the fire, against Nate. Oliver had fallen asleep across their laps, his sandy hair flopping over his tiny forehead. The parlor was atypically quiet because Leo and Tess had been permitted to play in the attic today, an infrequent and coveted treat. "Who sent you a letter on Christmas Eve? Anyone…special?"

Unfortunately, yes. But not in the way Cora hoped.

Gavin frowned at the letter. He didn't recognize the handwriting, but he did recognize the addressor. *Mr. Serjeant B. Norwood*

The very last thing Gavin wanted on Christmas Eve was a letter from Bartholomew Norwood, marked with a seal blatantly advertising his important rank.

Damn it.

"Thank you, Coates," he muttered, stuffing the letter in his pocket. "I'll see to it later."

A light knock sounded at the parlor door. "Mrs. Travers, will you need me for Leo this afternoon?"

Emilia stood in the threshold with her hooded cloak draped over her arm. Gavin stared at the garment with something akin to mourning. His hand nearly spasmed, as if his skin and bones retained the precise sensation of sliding beneath the heavy wool to find the taut expanse of her stomach.

"Oh no, Miss Davis. It's Christmas Eve. You don't need to work today." Cora took in Emilia's cloak. "Is there somewhere you want to go?"

"I was hoping to go into town." Emilia smiled prettily, and

Gavin's elbow inadvertently knocked into the chessboard. "I'd like to buy the children each a Christmas present."

"Oh, that's wonderfully thoughtful but unnecessary," Cora began. "You don't need to do that—"

"I know. But I'd like to," Emilia insisted. "And I haven't seen the town yet."

"It's small but quaint." Cora smiled, absently stroking Oliver's back. "It's not a market day, but I'm sure given the holiday, it will be lovely and festive. If I didn't need to ready myself for the Wallaces' Christmas Eve party tonight, I would join you."

"Sinclair will join you," Nate said casually.

What?

"What?"

Gavin looked at Nate in alarm. He had one arm resting along the back of the settee, his fingers lazily stroking the ends of Cora's hair, which made him seem doting and attentive; in truth, he was a criminal mastermind.

Nate shrugged. "You don't mind, do you, Sinclair?" He paused, as if relishing his next words. "You could take the sleigh."

Gavin had feared Nate would be a problem, and he'd been right.

"Oh!" Emilia went pale. "That's not—"

"I don't need to go," Gavin said quickly. "In fact, I'd prefer to stay here. I have some notes to review before the Wallaces' party."

"But Miss Davis has never seen town. She'll appreciate an escort, Gavin." Cora looked flummoxed. "And the sleigh would be charming on Christmas Eve."

"Yes." Nate grinned at Gavin. "Miss Davis has never seen town, Sinclair. She would miss out on its charm."

Gavin gritted his jaw. "A word, Travers?"

Nate unhurriedly kissed Oliver's knuckles and maneuvered the sleeping child fully onto Cora's lap. He stood and stretched before following Gavin to the corridor, feigning nonchalance.

"What, may I ask, are you doing?" Gavin glared.

Nate smirked. "What, may I ask, are you *not* doing?"

Gavin huffed impatiently. "I'm not engaging in this nonsense. Speak plainly. The women are waiting."

"So gallant, Sinclair," Nate observed merrily. "I wouldn't have expected such chivalry from a man lusting over my son's new governess."

"I—ah. What…ah…" Gavin suddenly had a blazing headache. "That's not…accurate," he finished lamely.

"Wait a moment." Nate looked delighted. "Are you playing coy about this?"

Yes. "There's nothing to be coy about," Gavin said. "Nothing has transpired…"

Nate eyed him expectantly, but Gavin wouldn't divulge their secret. Emilia asked him not to.

"Nothing has transpired," he repeated with conviction. "Between Miss Davis and me."

"Right," Nate said slowly. He looked at Gavin for a long time. "You've put me in a tricky position, Sinclair."

"Hardly—"

"My wife is quite taken with Miss Davis. She's already attached, you see. I cannot permit you to court my governess—"

"I assure you, that won't be a prob—"

"Badly," Nate finished. "I cannot permit you to court her *badly*. Which it appears you are in imminent danger of doing." He crossed his arms. "Cora won't want to hire a new governess, but I wager the sting will be severely lessened if she's hosting your wedding breakfast instead."

Gavin stared at Nate. "There's no wedding."

"Which brings us back to the terrible courting."

Gavin heaved a sigh, his shoulders sagging. "What do you know?"

"Only that you've been staring at her for five days." Nate started counting on his fingers. "You've been distracted and tetchy and haven't paid attention to a word from anyone but Miss Davis, who, I might add, is being *oddly* stingy with her words to you, and *only* to you. She blushes every time you walk in a room. It's nauseating…and quite charming." Nate paused. "You know, Cora and I were much more discreet."

Gavin gave him a pointed look. "Travers, I know you mean well, but you need to just let me handle this." He shook his head. "You don't understand."

"Nor do I want to," Nate said, raising a shoulder. "I'm only saying we have a sleigh. And Miss Davis wants to go to the shops. And my family will be *here*, not bothering you."

Gavin exhaled, thinking it over. Would it be so terrible to be snug in a sleigh with Emilia, and only Emilia?

No.

And yes.

"Fine," he relented. "I suppose it would be impolite to not escort Miss Davis to the shops."

"Horridly impolite," Nate agreed, turning to the door.

"Travers—"

"Fear not, Sinclair. I won't breathe a word to Cora."

Gavin scrubbed a hand over face, then reluctantly followed Nate.

Emilia was waiting in the parlor. She looked painfully lovely with her blue cloak and her gold hair and her pink cheeks.

Gavin squared his shoulders.

Don't look down.

8

____

Emilia had gotten her wish. She was being whisked along in a
horse-drawn sleigh with a handsome man, cozy under a fur blanket, her boots against a footwarmer. The snow-stippled woods
were dazzling, the muted evergreens and towering oaks brightened by the sticky red buds of horse chestnuts and the silvery bark
of birch trees.

But she didn't feel very merry.

They weren't speaking. The only sound was the horse's hooves,
crunching over well-packed snow, and the occasional trill of a blue
tit, its wings flashing bright through the trees. Gavin sat stiffly
beside her, his gloved hands holding the horse's reins in his lap.
He had given the full mantle of heavy fur to Emilia.

Her heart lurched at how miserably uncomfortable he looked,
wrapped only in a great coat.

At the Belle, he'd told her he was used to being quiet. So
perhaps this brittling silence was no hardship for him. But…he *had*
spoken to her that night. He'd been reserved in name only, joining
her silly game, sharing about his family.

What had he told her? *You're listening to me.*

Emilia hated this tension between them. She was sick to death of it. How many things had he wanted to say in the last five days that nobody heard? It was Christmas Eve. They were taking a sleigh ride in the snow, and nobody could overhear them.

And blast it…she *wanted* to listen to him.

She looked at Gavin, and found his gaze was on her, wary and soft.

"What?" she asked uncertainly.

"Are you warm enough?"

"Oh." The question surprised her. "Yes, this is quite lovely." She smiled. "Though I'm used to a chill."

He made an afflicted sound, deep in his throat. "Would you like my scarf?"

"No." She laughed lightly. "You'll freeze. Don't think of me. I'm fine."

He regarded her. "Are you though?"

She tilted her head.

"You don't necessarily seem fine. You're quiet," he observed. "You're quieter now than at any time since I met you."

She'd been thinking the same. How fantastically wretched, to be in stride yet still so far apart.

"I'm not sure what we're allowed to talk about," she admitted. "This is more difficult than I expected it to be. The not speaking to you." *The putting you behind me.*

Gavin looked down, a lock of hair curling over his forehead. Beneath his beaver hat, his ears were pink from cold. It was impossible to tell whether he was blushing or not. Emilia sensed he was.

"It doesn't have to be difficult." His voice was soft. "It wasn't difficult before, Emilia."

"Miss Davis," she reluctantly corrected.

He was silent for a beat, then he roughly shook his head. "No."

"No?"

"I won't call you Miss Davis." He set his jaw, doubling down on this small act of rebellion. "Emilia is the name you gave me at the Belle. You said we weren't strangers when you gave it to me. And…" He turned to face her. "I don't want to give it back."

In the feeble December sun, his eyes seemed a brighter blue. The tenderness there filled her with a fearsome sense of longing.

Emilia realized that in all her vague fantasies, her dream house had been full of objects but never *her*. She had never dared to imagine her hands lifting the copper kettle, her feet tucking beneath the embroidered quilt. She had never dared to imagine opening the door to the sound of her own name. There was safety in her suppression; if she never voiced her desires, she couldn't be denied them.

But nor could she deny Gavin her name.

"You don't have to give it back," she murmured, her heart lifting high and light within her. "Nobody calls me by my given name. I've forgotten how much I like it."

He nodded, and it steeled her resolve. If he could be brave enough to demand her name, she could be brave enough to retract her wall.

"But what I *don't* like," she went on, clenching her gloved hands in her lap, "is this silence between us."

He loosened a tense sigh, his exhale crystallizing in the chill air. His frustration was a cloud, drifting between them.

"You asked for this," he finally said. "You said you wished to forget it happened."

"I did," she said softly. "I did say that."

He worked his jaw, his blue eyes flickering over her. "I'm not…*good* at this, Emilia." He frowned. "The closest I've ever come to being good at it was that evening with you. If you want us to talk, you need to tell me. I only want to respect your wishes."

"And here I was only trying to respect *you*." She looked down, flushing. "When I met you, I didn't know you were so important, so influential. That first evening…I suppose I wanted to be just a boy and a girl. Unburdened and at ease. But that was foolish. We are grown, and you have a big life—"

"I don't have a big life," he interjected. "Not at all. It was true, what I told you. I keep to myself. I keep my head down. My life... is quite small. It's essentially *only* my work. Work is all I do. My sole focus. It's made me wretched at everything else."

Emilia's chest ached. She lifted the fur and slid closer to him, draping it over his knees.

"You don't need to—"

"Hush." She waved aside his protest. "I can't sit here any longer watching you hunched up like that. I have warmth enough to spare."

His gaze roved her face. "Yes. You do."

"Now then..." She looked up at him, smiling expectantly. "Tell me about it. Your work."

"It's not..."

"You're a barrister," she prompted. "Do you enjoy it?"

He pondered the question. "I've had a number of successes."

"No." She lifted the corner of her mouth. "I asked do you *like* your work? Are you glad to be doing it?"

"Ah. That's a timely question." He laughed humorlessly. "I suppose...I don't really have the luxury to feel glad about it. I have to earn a living somehow."

He grew contemplative.

"People are complicated, and they do complicated things. The law tries to make order of it, but that can be complicated too. I try to do right by others." He shook his head, staring at her intently. "I need to do better."

"Are you working on something now?" She was curious. It was a pleasurable puzzle, to ask him questions, to keep him talking.

"Yes." He rolled his shoulders. "That is, I'm *considering* taking on a brief. I have to decide by the new year."

"It's a hard decision?"

"Yes. It's a nightmare, actually." He studied a line of evergreens as the horse trotted over the flattened swathes of snow. "On one hand, this case could open a door for me, a door I very much wish would open. A tremendous opportunity for my own prospects. I could help many people...one day."

"Well then, that's good, isn't it? Why can't you open it?"

He briefly closed his eyes. "Because it would be at the price of my ethics. My character isn't something I ever thought would be for sale...but I'm at a loss, Emilia. My *not* taking this brief will likely put me out of favor with some important people. My *taking* the brief means the promotion I've worked for is tainted. Worst of all, it could be quite damaging..." His expression was pained as he looked at her. "It could be quite damaging for someone who is very vulnerable. No matter what I do, it's going to cause harm."

She was gratified that he'd opened up to her; he was plainly twisted in knots. But wasn't that the answer he needed? Not many men took such consideration when power and wealth were on offer.

Before she could think better of it, she reached for his arm. They were both wearing fur-lined gloves, and she couldn't feel him the way she wished. But even this veiled touch was enough to bridge the chasm that had opened. The solid weight of his forearm under her palm was a tether. She wasn't above her life. She was inside it.

And for the first time, she wanted to be right where she was.

"I don't think you would cause harm," she said softly.

"Is that so?"

He looked so sadly sincere. She wanted to unbury his smile.

"Well, I can certainly speak to your character. It's above reproach." She peeked at him slyly. "Not even a strange woman at an inn could besmirch it. Believe me, she tried."

He chuckled, warm and unexpected, and the sound of his humor set Emilia aglow.

"She did try," he mused. "Perhaps you're right."

"I usually am." She shrugged modestly, then grinned. "I imagine that's difficult for you."

"You can be right," he murmured, his mouth quirking up in a slow smile. "I don't need to be right."

"Fine." She raised her eyebrow. "Be wrong."

His jaw ticked once, a faint, lovely little battle on his face, and then he had his arm around her, pulling her closer beneath the blanket. His leg was pinned against her thigh, their sides pressed together.

"Just in case," he said casually, looking over the snowy woods. "I'd hate for you to feel the chill."

Her heartbeat crashed to the point of pain. "Suddenly, you're worrying over me?"

She'd meant to tease, but his gaze was heavy.

"Something like that."

He looped the reins and slid his free hand beneath the fur mantle, finding her hand under the blanket. Slowly, he laced their gloved fingers together. She was held fast against him, and it should have felt snug, but all Emilia could feel was a sharp crackle between them.

His fingers dipped between hers, gently tracing back and forth. She was acutely aware of the slight lurch of the sleigh, how the sway settled between her hips, how her hips pressed to Gavin's beneath the blanket where he played with her fingers.

She wished she hadn't mentioned the inn and the besmirching of honor.

"And you?" His voice was low against her ear. "Do you have complicated feelings about your work?"

Emilia watched the blue tit alight on a branch and tried to likewise settle her heart, which was no longer only beating within her chest. A shuddering ache pounded in her wrists, her throat, deep and high between her thighs. The restless pressure had her spreading her knees, just a little, under the blanket.

A bit ago they hadn't been speaking. Look how much changed when they got out of their blasted heads. Everything was looser. She felt reckless and safe, all at once.

"I like my work," she said slowly, wanting to be as honest as he had been. "I enjoy teaching. I love how children just…accept you. I feel most like myself when I'm with them. But it's not easy…in fact, it's quite isolating. I feel like I'm always trying to fit inside a box that wasn't meant for me."

Gavin hummed softly in her ear, a soothing murmur of acknowledgment. She turned her hand over in his, and he wordlessly slid one finger beneath her sleeve, his leather fingertip drawing patterns on the inside of her wrist. Emilia's whole body tingled with the decadence of this simple contact. She loved being cradled by him, her head on his wool-clad shoulder. She loved the way he stroked her hand and wrist. She loved being touched in any way at all.

"It's hard for me to find work," she admitted. "My parents left me with very little money. There was just enough to pay for a boarding school education, but I could never afford the extras— foreign languages, music, etiquette. I lack the skills that could set me up in the homes of Mayfair, preparing fine young ladies for society. So I have to make the best of being a nursery governess." She sighed. "Teaching young children means I must frequently find new work. Always starting over is difficult."

"Your family?" His voice was a soft exhale on her cheek. His thigh was warm and solid against hers. It was astonishing, really, how all of the touching made the hard things easier.

Emilia shook her head, and his head moved with her. "No…not really. Not anymore. My second cousin is alive; he took me in for a spell when I was young. It wasn't a good situation. He is very callous." Emilia's stomach clenched. Gavin kept her steady with the soothing trail of his fingers, back and forth on the inside of her wrist. "So I went away to school…and that's another type of cold. I had some friends, sometimes, but they had families to return to and I didn't. So. You know."

"I don't, Emilia." He shifted, and she turned to face him. His expression was at once thunderous and somber. His hand laced with hers again, and he squeezed hard. "I don't know at all."

"Don't pity me," she warned. "I don't care for that."

He shook his head. "Pity you? My God. I *admire* you. Your resilience, your good humor. And here you are complimenting *my* character."

Her eyes were suddenly wet and stinging in the cold. "I try," she admitted.

"That's so much more than most people do." His hand came to her face, and she closed her eyes. He gently pressed a fingertip to her lashes, his glove soaking up her tears before they could freeze.

A faint, hovering breath.

And then his mouth was over her eyelids. Warm, soft, easing the sting.

She tilted her face.

She wanted him to kiss her. She had never wanted anything so much.

She put her gloved hand to his mouth, and he groaned softly. She traced his lips, and then he was yanking off his glove, and his finger was inside *her* glove, deftly working the leather away from her wrist. His bare fingertip teased the exposed, delicate skin of her hand, and she gasped.

"I'm sorry. I know it's cold," he muttered. "I've just…I've been wanting to touch you again…"

She was shifting restlessly, her knees now wide against his beneath the blanket. Gavin slid his boot behind her calf, pressing their shins together, angling her body closer to his. Emilia lifted her free hand to his face, pulling him to her. Their foreheads touched, and then, with a frustrated groan, he dropped his bare thumb to her bottom lip, dragging over it until she opened her mouth, his parted lips just brushing hers—

The horse snorted, the reins jostling in Gavin's lap. The sleigh lurched and he cursed, pulling away from her to snatch the tether.

"I have to drive." He sounded shocked by the notion. "*Hell*. We could have ended up in the bloody trees!"

At the outrage on his face, Emilia started laughing again—so big and loud, it frightened away the poor blue tit.

"Is this putting it behind us?" she managed to ask, pressing her hand over her mouth as another laugh bubbled.

"No," he said, shaking his head, smiling at her laugh. "It's not."

"Gavin..." she said, drawing a breath, her laughter subsiding. "It keeps happening."

"Yes."

"What do we do?"

At that moment, the woods thinned, and the bustling town came into view. Gavin looked at her and shrugged helplessly.

"We go Christmas shopping."

9

———

Cora's local town was a far cry from the city clamor Gavin was accustomed to, but there was nevertheless an air of anticipation as folk hurried to finish errands before the holiday. Wreaths hung on doors, candles gleamed in windows, and passersby called jovial greetings. As he strolled through the quaint square with Emilia, Gavin appreciated anew that today was Christmas Eve. He'd clearly lost the thread of time and place in the sleigh, what with her being so happy and breathy and warm beneath the blanket.

Emilia, too, was winsomely caught up in the festive atmosphere. Her unbridled enthusiasm was so catching that Gavin, who had never enjoyed visiting shops a day in his life, was very much enjoying it today. Together, they explored, peeking into the baker's and the chandler's, wandering through the stationer's, where Emilia fussed over a selection of pressed bookmarks. Gavin had already completed his purchases in London—he tended to give everyone books—but he liked watching her peruse the offerings, her face alight as she considered each option.

And then they went to the grocer, where it all went to hell.

Gavin had never considered a town grocer to be an establishment where erotic fantasies were born. A grave mistake, on his part. If he had known what awaited him, he might have shored up his defenses, which were already weak from the near-kiss in the sleigh. He could still feel the exquisite softness of Emilia's wrist beneath his finger.

It was only a matter of time before he came undone.

He just hadn't expected peppermint to do it.

Emilia was leaning over the counter, peering into tall glass jars filled with sweets and choosing selections for Leo—barley sugar candies, lemon drops, lozenges of licorice.

She was also, at that moment, sampling a peppermint stick, which Gavin would now decry as dangerous contraband in a court of law.

The peppermint had innocent origins; it was given to her by the kindly grocer when he noticed her wide-eyed delight at the treat. She'd taken the candy and unwrapped the paper, admiring the cheerful red stripe. "Look how festive!"

But then the entire operation was assailed by an onslaught so unexpectedly sensual, it had Gavin clenching his fist hard enough to pop the veins in his forearm.

He stood to the side of the counter, breathing through his nose, trying to put his gaze anywhere except the sweet hollow of Emilia's lips as they wrapped around the peppermint stick with a sinful pop.

For the love of *Christ*. He was fighting his first public cockstand since he'd been a lad at Harrow. And he might be losing.

He chanced a look at her at the same moment she moved the peppermint to the corner of her mouth. His jaw grew slack at the flash of her tongue, idly lapping the column of candy.

Gavin was a well-educated man; he'd been blessed with a sharp mind and the opportunities to cultivate it. But right now, he had no thoughts except *sugar* and *mouth* and *lips* and *Emilia*.

"It really does melt on the tongue," she marveled to the grocer.

That's it. Gavin threw a handful of pennies on the counter. "Box up whatever she selects," he muttered. "I'll be outside."

He stepped into the street, leaving the warmth and peppermint and pink lips behind him. He needed to clear his head and cool his blood.

As good a time as any for opening the letter he'd been ignoring all day.

He reached into his great coat and withdrew Norwood's correspondence. This letter made him uneasy. Norwood shouldn't be writing to him directly; he should go through his solicitor. Gavin found his spectacles, eased open the seal, and scanned the contents. There was a note and a newspaper clipping from *The Times*, dated two days ago. It was the gossip column and had been underlined with a heavy hand.

The tale of the Gaudy Governess continues. Last evening, Mr. Samuel Norwood was overheard at his club, warning a gentleman off hiring Miss Charity Matthews, who, according to rumor, hasn't worked since she pressed a breach of promise suit against him. According to the young buck, the Adventuress swindled him twice—first in his heart and now in his (very heavy!) pocketbook. But fear not, Reader, Mr. Norwood's future is in good hands, what with his well-connected father hinting their defense counsel will be none other than Mr. Gavin Sinclair, the upstart barrister who has not lost a single trial since August.

The corresponding note was brief.

Sinclair: My family is in Berkshire visiting a cousin for Christmastide, coincidentally not far from your sister's residence of Aldworth Park. Shall we meet to discuss your prospects? My son would be fortunate indeed if these rumors turn out to be true.

Gavin groaned in frustration. He absolutely had not yet accepted the case. The fact that Samuel Norwood was blasting the news all over London only tangled the knot tighter. Not to mention Miss Matthews, who was being raked over the coals, just as Gavin had feared.

His head pounded as he thought of Emilia. *It's hard for me to find work. It's difficult to always start over.* Unpleasant questions rattled through him. Miss Matthews was...where? Boarding somewhere? Did she have family? What would happen to her if she didn't win her suit?

What is Norwood thinking? The serjeant was presently in Berkshire, and he wanted to meet. It was highly frowned upon for a client and barrister to meet without a solicitor. It just wasn't done. Norwood either assumed Gavin to be so ambitious as to be swayed by a powerful connection, or he thought Gavin was weak, someone he could buy and sell to do his family's bidding.

But Gavin only wanted to do the *right* thing.

He shoved the letter in his pocket and resolved to put it out of his mind. There was nothing he could do about any of this on Christmas Eve.

Besides, he had enough trouble at present, what with the woman he was courting…badly.

By the time Emilia emerged from the grocer's with a small wrapped parcel, she was blessedly peppermint-free and Gavin had regained his faculties.

"What a lovely shop," she said merrily. She held his coins in her gloved hand. "Here you are. I won't allow you to purchase my gifts for me. And you drastically overpaid." She looked him up and down. "Are you feeling well?"

"I'm fine." He straightened his coat. "I just needed some air. Where to next?"

"The haberdasher," she said decisively. "I'd like to find a hair ribbon for Tess."

Thankfully, the haberdasher had no illicit sweets nor unsavory news. It did, however, have more fabric-related accoutrements than Gavin had ever conceived of in his life.

Emilia cooed over a pale blue lace ribbon. "Look—it matches her eyes!"

Gavin dubiously eyed the lace. "A bit fragile for Tess."

Emilia pursed her lips and reconsidered the blue lace. "Too right. She needs something fancy but sturdy."

The proprietor directed her to a display of satin in the back corner.

"I think this must be more fun than receiving a present," Emilia mused as she gently trailed a fingertip over scraps of ribbon. "Choosing something for someone else, wondering how they'll react. I'm glad I'll be able to see it."

"Did you have a favorite Christmas present?" Gavin asked, watching her admire the colorful display.

"Oh…no." Emilia shook her head thoughtfully. "Actually, now that you mention it, I can't remember ever having been given a Christmas present."

"What?" Gavin stopped short, appalled. "What do you mean you never had a present? In your *life*?"

She looked at him askance. "I told you I have no family. Who on earth would have given me a present?"

Gavin stared at her, but Emilia chattered away, oblivious to the fact that her pronouncement made him want to destroy something.

"You know, my first holiday at Miss Prestwick's school—I was eleven or twelve years old—one of the girls, Bess, came back from Christmas with the most divine peach ribbon. I think I may have *curdled* with envy." She smiled faintly. "Can you imagine? Bess used to permit me to hold it in the evenings before she packed it away. Isn't that marvelously tragic?" She shrugged. "I haven't thought about it in years."

"Emilia…"

Gavin's chest was constricting so tightly, it bruised to breathe. All the pieces of what he knew of her were falling into place like so many wind-drunk flakes of snow. She had never been to a Christmas party. She had no family. She traveled alone, on a bloody *mail coach*.

She'd never unwrapped a parcel selected especially for her.

No. Absolutely not.

"Choose a hair ribbon," he said before he realized what he was thinking. "Choose ten. Whatever you like."

He heard his words and winced. *For the love of God on high.* Gavin couldn't even give a present correctly. He didn't want to give her a bloody *hair ribbon.*

But Emilia had turned pink and dimply, and he all at once felt he'd had the best idea in the world.

"Oh, you don't have to do that." She laughed, full and bright, a rush of joy from her stomach to his. "Gavin, no. We're choosing presents for the children—"

"And you." He caught her hand, paying no mind to the shopkeeper. "And *you,* Emilia."

He guided her hand to the display, spreading her fingers over the ribbons. They had both removed their thick gloves in the warm shop, and he couldn't stop his thumb from tracing the ridge of her chapped knuckles.

"You could have the blue lace," he murmured. "You can handle fragile things."

"Try it, miss," the proprietor urged. "Go on. It's Christmas Eve."

"My hair is already pinned." Emilia shook her head. She lifted the ribbon, letting it unfurl around her fingers. "It's enough…just to know I have it."

"You needn't use it for your hair," the shopkeeper said, clearly intent on making a sale. "Most women don't."

"That's true." Emilia mused, still stroking the ribbon. "I could weave it into a basket. Or tie my stockings—"

She broke off, flushing, and Gavin choked back a groan at the thought of blue lace high beneath her skirts. For an interminable moment, she stared at him with those beautiful, amber-flecked eyes, and his nerves dissipated in a frisson of possibility. He felt the most inordinate sense of calm when she looked at him like that. Like he could do anything and he wouldn't have to think about it first.

He took the end of the ribbon and pulled, letting it slide from her fingers to his. She watched it trail between them, her dark lashes lowered.

"If you two will excuse me just a moment," the shopkeeper said, clearly oblivious to the tension blooming between his patrons. "I need to nip to the stockroom."

Gavin hardly heard the man. He hadn't heard a single word since Emilia speculated that this ribbon might tighten around her thigh.

"Turn around," he murmured the moment they were alone. His palms curved over her shoulders.

"I...what?" She was staring at his mouth. No, lower than his mouth. His chin. "What are you doing? You heard what he said. Women don't wear them like this—"

"Turn around," Gavin instructed, slowly rotating her. "What does it matter what other women do? It's yours. Would you like to wear this ribbon in your hair?"

She laughed, her whole face luminous. "Yes, I would."

"Then we should see if it suits."

He lifted the ribbon to her heavy coil of golden hair. A few tendrils had come free, trailing her nape, and he touched her there, gently winding a loose lock around his finger.

"Ooh," she crooned as his fingers flexed, slightly loosening her pinned hair bun.

"So soft," he muttered. "I wondered."

He felt vaguely, dangerously unhinged. How long would her hair be if he unpinned it all right now? He'd been wondering for a week.

Instead, he gathered the knot in his hand, wrapping the ribbon around it and carefully tying the blue lace.

"Does it look nice?" She craned her neck. "I suppose I need a mirror."

"Lovely," he murmured. "I wish you could see how lovely."

She reached back, her fingers skimming her neck, then her coiffure, gently touching the ribbon. "It *feels* lovely. Thank you—"

And then, because they were still alone, because it was *too much* —too soft and golden and aching and sweet—he ducked his head and pressed his mouth to the back of her exposed neck.

She gasped sharply, her dimple retreating as her mouth dropped into a round of surprise. She froze, holding herself still, but when he kissed her neck again, she shuddered and sank into him.

He put his arms around her, bracing them next to hers on the counter, bracketing her against him. He nosed the back of her hair, his breath hot on her nape. Emilia's hands came up over his, her fingernails trailing up and down his arms. Gavin desperately wished he weren't wearing a wool overcoat, that he could feel her touching him. But it was no matter, because the only skin he cared about was *hers*—the sweet stretch of neck between the collar of her cloak and her ear, a perfect trail for his tongue, for his lips.

"*Gavin…*"

Her breath was strained. He could hardly peel himself away from her, not with her feathering plea in his ears. Gone were his mild mannerisms—they were melting away, turning to ash, curling into smoky, blackened edges of kindling. His honorable intentions were no better than soft wood whose only purpose was to nurture flames.

In the distance came the sound of a door latching, of footsteps echoing.

Gavin closed his eyes and took one step back, then another. Emilia stood frozen, her hands on the counter, her head bowed, her color high. The blue ribbon fluttered against her neck, where Gavin's mouth had just been.

"Did you make a selection?" The shopkeeper asked, bustling behind the counter.

"We'll…we'll take the blue." She put her hand vaguely to her hair, her dark eyes glassy. "Here, let me give it to you, so you can wrap it with the others."

Gavin thrust a coin in the till. He felt as if he were making this purchase from underwater, so sluggish and distracted was he. "She can continue wearing it," he rasped to the shopkeeper. "No need to wrap it."

"Happy Christmas," the haberdasher called as they made their way to the door. "Enjoy your evening."

Evening? Gavin startled. Sure enough, the sun was easing low in a purpling sky. The jarring awareness that the afternoon was waning finally pulled him back to himself.

He hastened for his pocket watch and flinched; it was nearly half past three.

"*Shite.*" Gavin closed his eyes. "I forgot. I'm invited to that bloody party at the Wallaces' tonight. Nate and Cora's friends… they always have a Christmas Eve celebration."

He dragged his hands through his hair, then checked his pocket watch again, as if it may have been tricking him before. "I'm expected soon. And by soon, I mean now. They start the festivities early. It's a whole damn nuisance."

Emilia put a hand on his forearm.

"You should go. I have a few more errands, but I don't want you to be late on my account."

"Emilia—"

"Take the sleigh," she urged. "I can finish here, then I'll wait in town. You can send a groom for me."

Gavin felt uneasy. It wasn't dark yet, but it would be soon. "I'm not going to leave you here."

"It's fine." she smiled reassuringly. "I'm perfectly capable of looking after myself, but you can't keep everyone waiting. I'll see you back at Aldworth Park."

He frowned. "I don't think so. Can't you come now?"

She shook her head. "I really need to attend to some matters here. Please, go back. Mrs. Travers will be waiting."

Gavin rocked on his heels. A groom could be here within an hour. Emilia would be back at Aldworth Park before he was even finished with predinner drinks at the Wallace home. *Hell.* All those people…he hated the thought of arriving late and causing a scene.

He heaved a tense sigh. "Fine. Yes. I'll send a groom. You'll wait here? In the square?"

She touched his cheek, then his chin. She pressed her little finger there and smiled. "Yes. Right here."

"I'll see you soon." Gavin thrummed with agitation and longing. He had a burning and imprecise sense of what he wanted—Emilia in his arms, her hair unpinned, his mouth against her neck while she told him of herself, of her life, of all the ways he could care for her.

He looked her over, and abruptly shrugged out of his scarf, winding it around her blue-cloaked shoulders.

"Gavin—"

"I won't leave you cold," he said. "Not again."

And then he brushed his mouth over her gloved knuckles and turned for the sleigh.

10

——————

Emilia watched Gavin depart, the imprint of his mouth still on her neck, beneath his scarf. What just happened? What had been happening all day? *All week?*

If the shopkeeper hadn't returned, if they had remained alone, Emilia would have given herself to him. She knew this without question. She would have let him lift her skirts, she would have let him press his body against hers, she would have let him put his hands anywhere he wanted…because she wanted it too.

Her stomach clenched, a vise funneling pinpricks of heat to her extremities. Emilia had felt desire before, quickened by a passage in a novel or the broad shoulders of a farmhand who worked for the Grangers. She clung to these half-formed fantasies when she was alone, using her own hand to curb her restless ache.

This…with Gavin…was not like that. This desire wasn't aimless or vague. It was heavy. It was focused. It belonged to him.

Am I in over my head?

Yes. Assuredly, she was in over her head. It was, in truth, partly why she stayed in town. She felt hot and delicate and needed a moment to herself. If they were in the sleigh together, beneath the blanket, alone…

Emilia tipped back her head, as if to upend her fevered thoughts and spill them sizzling into the snow. But turning her face skyward was hardly a help. It was nearing dusk, and that rare blue seemed to taunt her through the gathering clouds.

She took her time finishing her shopping—a small bar of scented soap for Annie, a new pair of wool stockings for herself—and then she hesitated. She wanted to find something for Gavin. At week's end, he would return to London, and while she didn't understand the scope of what stretched between them, she understood it was fragile enough to break at the end of the holidays.

He had a life to return to, and she had a life to build here.

She meant what she told him in the sleigh—she liked her work. Not only because of the children, but because of the *purpose*. It mattered to her, to matter. Perhaps it was a frivolous thing to want when *so much* was wanting, but she couldn't stop herself.

She wanted to matter to Gavin Sinclair.

Now, she looked over a selection of stationery. Perhaps he would like that? He was always taking notes. She considered heavy sheets of parchment before moving to the next display, a small assortment of quill pens. She lifted a goose feather quill, remembering his fervent whisper, *You have me breaking quills.*

But Gavin was a good man. He wouldn't break something she gave him.

She paid for the quill and waited as the shopkeeper packaged it for her. That handled, she stepped back into the cold.

She had no watch, and she didn't know the time. She wandered past the church; the doors were closed, but tomorrow morning, the bells would ring for Christmas Day. From across the green came the sounds of carolers, going door to door. She listened for a moment, then laughed. "The Twelve Days of Christmas."

It suddenly seemed nonsensical to wait idly, as if she were a fair lady who needed to be fetched. She didn't want a footman or groom to have to come for her on Christmas Eve. Emilia had been looking after herself her whole life; she could surely see herself to

Aldworth Park. Gavin had taken all the parcels except the small ones she'd procured after his departure. They easily fit in the concealed pocket in her bodice.

It would be a bit of a hike, but that was no matter. She was wearing her hooded cloak and her hobnail boots, and the bridle paths were comprised of well-packed snow. She rather relished the idea of a walk to settle herself before she saw him again.

She would benefit from some *settling*.

Besides, the Traverses and Gavin would be at their friends' Christmas party. The children would be readying for bed. It's not as though anyone was expecting her.

The notion of inconveniencing this new household made her deeply uncomfortable. Everyone had been so kind; not just the family, but the servants as well. She didn't want to overstep and make demands on anyone's time, not when she could walk on her two perfectly good feet. How many times had she trekked to town and back with Robbie Granger?

Her mind made up, she headed toward the bridle path, briskly striding in the lovely frosted wood, following the tracks of the sleigh. A light snow had started falling. It twirled against the darkening sky, fine as spun sugar. The ephemeral flakes would not gather, too fragile to accumulate into any sort of substance. This was the sort of snow that would kiss the ground and fade away.

As she walked, she watched the swirling flakes. They sought purchase time and again, only to be denied.

Fall and fade, fall and fade.

She touched Gavin's quill, tucked safe in her bodice.

Emilia knew what she would keep, if she could keep anything in the world.

HE'D MADE A MISTAKE. The moment he stepped foot inside the Wallaces' grand estate, Gavin regretted it. This wasn't where he wanted to be—rubbing elbows with Cora and Nate's friends, all of whom had no interest in Gavin aside from prattling on about his pending promotion.

He wanted to be quiet and still with Emilia.

He suffered through drinks in Lady Wallace's resplendent drawing room, but as dinner loomed, his agitation was such, he knew he had to leave. Gavin wasn't one to be rude, but for once, he didn't give a damn what anyone else thought.

He'd spent the last half hour staring out the window, watching the lightly swirling snow. It seemed mild, but the fact that it was falling in the first place was enough to put his teeth on edge.

He'd left Emilia behind like a bloody idiot.

There was no conceivable way he could sit through a three-course dinner and the attendant card games and revelry. He had to make sure she was home.

Gavin finally found Nate and Cora and made his excuses—*a long day, a headache, he'd send the carriage back for them, enjoy, Happy Christmas.* It wasn't a hard negotiation. Cora was suspiciously bright, and Nate's waistcoat was buttoned askew; clearly, they had availed themselves of Lady Wallace's copious boughs of mistletoe.

Gavin took the carriage back to Aldworth Park, checking his pocket watch and feeling comforted that at least Thomas, the groom, had set out straight away to fetch Emilia. By now, she should be in her room, hopefully taking a hot bath…

And then what, he didn't know.

He damn well hoped he'd be lucky enough to find out.

But when he arrived, Thomas was pacing in the entry hall. The groom was snow-dusted and disconcerted.

And he was alone.

"Thomas?" Gavin narrowed his eyes, shaking snow off his hat. "Is something amiss?"

"I'm sorry, sir." Thomas winced, and Gavin immediately experienced a presage of dread.

"Why are you sorry?" Gavin cast his eyes about the hall.

"I asked around…most shops were closed," Thomas explained hastily. "But I checked where I could, and the main roadway too. I can go back out on horseback…if she took a bridle path."

Gavin stared at Thomas. He couldn't understand what the groom was saying.

"What do you mean? Speak plainly." His tone was taut. "Where, exactly, is Miss Davis?"

"I…I don't know, Mr. Sinclair." Thomas exhaled, looking outside. "I couldn't find her."

Gavin's heart wasn't beating correctly. It thundered unevenly; it clogged his ears.

"You couldn't find her."

"No, sir." Thomas hesitated.

Gavin turned the words over, looking for how to interpret the sentence in a way that meant Emilia was upstairs in a bath.

"You couldn't *find* her? So she's…not here?"

"No, sir."

"She's *outdoors*?"

"I can go back out—"

"Damn right you are going back out!" Gavin's voice sounded wrong. The words were sharp and loud, and he vaguely understood it was because he was shouting. Outside of cricket at Harrow, he had never shouted in his life.

He whirled around to the front window, taking in the cold dark sky.

This was his fault. *Jesus Christ*, what was wrong with him? Because of a party, he'd done this. Because of an obligation that didn't even matter.

How much of his life had he wasted on *bloody expectations*?

He turned to Thomas. "You're going out. I'm going out. I don't care *who* goes out!"

He strode to the door, flinging it open. He could think of nothing right now except Emilia's freezing room at the Belle. He hadn't slept that night, thinking of her alone and cold.

And now…now she was far more alone and far more cold.

Because of him.

"How long ago did you go out?" He started down the icy front steps, faintly illuminated by flickering torchlight. "How long, Thomas?"

His mind raced, trying to go through it. She should have been home by now…even walking, surely? *If* she walked.

If she didn't walk…where was she? Injured? Or had a fellow traveler picked her up? A beautiful woman, alone in the dark and snow…

A new horror altogether.

Damn it to hell.

"Mr. Sinclair…"

Thomas was jogging after him, and Gavin realized he was already partway down the sweep, still dressed in his evening clothes, hardly warm enough, but he couldn't bring himself to care.

"Mr. Sinclair, wait. We need a plan—"

"*You* make a plan. Go find Watts and make a plan. Find Coates, find Barnes, find Marlowe. I don't give a shite who you wake up or pull from their holiday. *You* do it, Thomas. I'm going out now."

"Gavin?"

Her voice. Behind him.

"Gavin, what on earth is going on?"

He spun around. Emilia was framed in the shadowed entry, looking at him. In blistering confusion, his feet propelled him to her, across the snowy sweep, up the front steps, and then he was upon her. He put his hands on her—her shoulders, her arms, her freezing hands.

He held her face, he looked at her face, her face was pink and her cheeks were cold, but she was in one piece.

"Where did you come from?"

"The kitchens." She stared at him in concern. "I came in

through the servants' passage, and I stopped there to warm up a bit. Then I heard you. Gavin, are you—"

He was no longer inside his body. He could feel his composure popping, splintering, caving beneath a tidal wave of relief and worry and guilt. "Get upstairs," he half growled. "Upstairs, right now."

"Gavin, I'm fine." Her dark eyes were wide. "Stop…whatever you're doing. I'm fine, I walked back. I didn't want anyone to have to bother—"

"I swear to heaven, Emilia, get upstairs, get out of those damp clothes, get in a bath. You could have frozen to death—"

"Gavin, I'm all right," she whispered. "Stop this. You're going to disturb everyone."

"I don't care." His voice was rough. "I don't care about *everyone*. I care about *you*."

He gripped her arm, he pulled her up the staircase, he tugged her down the corridor. But not to the third floor, where her room was, the second floor, where *his* room was, where a fire was lit and a bath was drawn because he'd asked Mrs. Bainsbridge to have both ready for his return, for that was the sort of methodical way he applied himself to life.

Until now.

He strode into his chambers and pulled her after him, slamming the door and storming over to the copper tub. The water was warm, but he yanked the kettle heating on the fireplace hob and upended it into the bath in a stream of steam.

"Back here, behind here." He dragged the privacy screen in front of the tub. "I won't look, but I need you to get in this bath."

"Gavin," she said quietly, "you don't need to worry. I'm just a little cold, but it's not so bad—"

He kept his back to her and crossed his arms. His head was pounding, even as he slowly began to understand she was right; she was safe. She was safe and warm in his room. With *him*, the idiot who put her in danger in the first place.

"Get in the bath, Emilia. You're freezing. Please." His hands raked through his hair. "Please just…"

Please let me do better.

"Fine," she murmured, clearly placating him since he'd become irrational. "Yes. All right."

He heard her moving behind the screen. There was a rustle of clothing followed by a quiet splash as she lowered herself into the steaming tub.

For a long moment, they were silent, both of them breathing hard. Gavin still had his hands in his hair. He was still looking at his closed chamber door.

He was realizing he was fucking insane.

"There. I'm in the bath." Her voice floated to him from behind the screen. "Now, you need to calm down, Gavin, and listen—"

"No." He spun to face the screen. Steam wafted from the tub, curling into the room. "No, you listen. It's *not* fine."

"I arrived here hale and whole. I know how to manage myself. I didn't want to put anyone out—"

"You were careless," Gavin said hoarsely. "You're careless with yourself because nobody has ever cared for you. You walked home in the dark in the middle of bloody winter *alone*. You traveled for days on a mail coach *alone*." As he said it, he comprehended anew just how precarious her situation had been. "Do Cora and Nate even know you took a mail coach, alone, in December? They would have sent a carriage to fetch you, Emilia. You didn't need to *meet* them. Why didn't you ask them?"

"Do you suppose anyone has *ever* sent a carriage to fetch me?" Her voice was sharp. "My last household terminated my employment with a *single day's* notice. They made no concessions for me. I *needed* this position. I took the mail coach because I could afford it and it wouldn't bother anybody. I walked home tonight because I don't mind walking." She huffed. "I can't…I can't just make demands of people."

"If anything had happened to you…" He choked back his frustration, his hands shaking at his sides. It was happening again, the mounting sense of defeat, that he'd gotten it wrong, that he'd let someone down, that he hadn't done enough.

"Gavin?"

His fault. He should be doing more.

"Gavin."

His ears were ringing; dread clawed up his neck. He stared at the screen, fighting for mastery over his shredding self-possession. He thought of how frigid her cheeks had felt beneath his palms.

*I would…*he realized. His blood rushed hot, and he wanted her to *feel* it. He wanted to press his heat upon her, upon all the many places where she'd long been steeped in cold. *I would make concessions for you.*

"Come here," she urged softly. "Come where I can see you. Please."

He was already coming around the screen, he was kneeling behind the tub, he was wrapping his arms around her wet shoulders. He pressed his face into her steam-softened hair. It was still pinned up; she was still wearing the blue ribbon. He breathed slowly, holding her against him, his elbows sinking into the bath. He sluiced his palms over her bare arms, her skin slick and warm. She had a line of freckles on her bicep. He traced it with his thumb, following the path to her shoulder.

Twice now, Gavin had walked away from her. Twice, her feet had carried her *here*, to where he was. She wouldn't stay where he left her. He didn't want her to.

Goddamn it. Gavin had been intent on following his own narrow path when he could have been following hers. This path here. The map of freckles on her shoulder.

"There. See? Nothing happened to me," Emilia murmured.

She turned her head and tugged his chin closer, until her forehead pressed to his. She touched his cheek, his mouth. Her skin smelled of soap. His fingers encircled her wrist, keeping her hand against his lips, nudging until her fingers opened, until he could kiss the center of her palm.

She unknotted his cravat, loosening the folds and resting her other hand on his collarbone. Her steady warmth eased the sting in his throat.

He could nearly find his breath. Nearly.

"Emilia," he managed. He traced her palm with his tongue, and she moaned. And that helped too.

"I'm here." She slipped her finger between his lips. "I'm right here."

He sucked hard, loving the weight of her finger on his tongue, how real and unyielding it was. Her moan hitched into a whine; her dusky lips dropped open.

He was all at once seized by the lack of her, unwilling to settle for her fingers, for the glistening slope of her shoulders. He wanted *her*. He wanted all of her. He wanted her to see she was enough for him, just as she was.

And then he was pulling her from the tub, warm water sloshing as she shifted, as he drew her into his lap. In the firelight, her body was wet and burnished. He reached for a towel and draped it around her. He held her flush to his chest, and his chest no longer hurt.

"I'm here," she repeated, her hands carding through his hair, turning it as damp as her own. He looked her over, the swell of her pink-tipped breasts, the curve of her calf. In the column of her throat, he could faintly see her pulse; it was very fast.

Surely, as fast as his.

She smiled, dimpled and exactly right, and his anxiety mounted into relief, then crested into something restless and enormous.

She was naked and wet and perfect on his lap, and the thread she'd been pulling all week was about to snap.

He pressed his lips to the juncture of her shoulder.

"At the inn, I stopped." His mouth worked across her shoulders and her neck, down her arm. *So soft.* He sucked her wrist, where her pulse shuddered. "I stopped kissing you."

"Yes," she whispered. "You did."

He was growing hard, instantly reacting to the sensation of her moving over him, to the sensation of *her*, just beyond her towel.

"Did you want me to?"

"No." She gripped his shoulders. "No, I did not want you to stop."

"My regret to bear." His throat felt thick; his nostrils flared. He couldn't look away from the damp, gleaming expanse of her. "I was trying to do the honorable thing."

"I thought you saw something in me you didn't like. That you changed your mind—"

He brought one hand to the back of her neck, his thumb brushing her pulse point, willing it to gentle for him. She sighed, heavy-lidded in the flickering light.

"Believe me," he breathed, leaning closer. "Emilia, it was never my intention to make you feel unwanted."

"You do want me?" Her dark eyes dilated. Her fingers slid back into his hair, burrowing in, holding tight.

"As if I were made for wanting you."

"This time...." She shuddered. Her lips parted; his nose nudged hers. "Don't stop."

His hand joined hers where the towel closed around her breasts. He kissed her there before pinning her with his gaze.

Gavin didn't need to look down to confirm this was the greatest leap of his life. He didn't need to look anywhere but at her.

"I'm not going to stop."

11

———

SHE HAD THOUGHT the tenderness between them was fragile, but there was nothing delicate about the hungry sweep of his mouth, nothing timid about the urgent press of his fingers. Gavin opened her towel and held her close, and when he touched her bare skin, she could see how this would go, how she wanted it to go, what she wanted to give him. His worry for her had been unbearable, but she would bear it. She would soothe him with the reality of her in his arms, in his bed.

Emilia moaned against his throat, relishing her own abandon. For how long had she endured boundless need, tamping down her futile longing? Now it was too much—surely, this excess of pleasure would incinerate her. She was the shimmering slick of air that floats above a flame, blurry and hazy, cresting the blaze.

Yes, yes, yes.

"Take your hair down." His voice scraped her ear. "Take it down, Emilia. Please."

She reached for her ribbon, her pins, and one by one, she pulled them free until her heavy hair fell past her shoulder blades. Gavin made a sound deep in his chest, and then his hands were everywhere, fisting and sifting through her damp tresses, his fingers flexing against her scalp, and the *tension*, the tension was—

"So good," he rasped. "My *God*, it's intolerable."

She was moving on his lap, she couldn't stop, not with him kissing her with such wicked, focused precision. Beneath her, his cock was a rigid pressure she could now see was meant for her, made so she could part her thighs and rock her rising need against it—*yes, harder*.

"Oh…"

"Emilia." He looked upon her, glazed and burning.

"Yes," she murmured, rolling her hips into his. "*Please.*"

"Wait. *Wait.*" He gently squeezed her arms, breathing hard. "Emilia…wait."

"What is it?"

He fell silent, his jaw tightening.

"Gavin?"

"I…I've never done this," he finally confessed, his cheeks turning pink in the fire glow.

"Done what?"

His flush deepened. "Ah…this."

It took her a moment to understand. "You…you've never?" She stroked the back of his neck.

"It just…never happened," he muttered. "Some of it has—the kissing. A bit more. But not often, and never…the rest of it." He gripped her hand tightly. "It always seemed a risk I couldn't take." He swallowed. "Until now."

Gavin's eyes were very dark, but she could see a flicker of nerves. Emilia's heart crashed in her chest, as if wanting to leave her body and go to him. Her perfectly careful man. The lengths he would go to for her.

For only her.

"Gavin, you needn't burden yourself with this," she said softly. "I have no expectations. I haven't any notions of this either."

"And that's why it matters." He walked his fingertips up and down her spine. "I want to make this very good for you."

She thought about the dedicated intensity of his kiss, of how he turned her lust-drunk with nothing more than teasing her wrist. When he'd pressed his mouth to her neck in the shop, she nearly swooned; she would have, if he hadn't been holding her.

"I sincerely believe you'll be just fine," she murmured, kissing the concern from his brow. "You're a very…diligent man."

"Diligent." The curve of his mouth tilted up, his jaw slowly relaxing.

"Very," she confirmed, tracing his lips.

"I do work hard…" He ducked his head, his warm breath ghosting along her neck. "I work *tirelessly* hard."

His lips recaptured hers. She welcomed the fervent onslaught, desperately meeting his mouth until she was boneless and torpid. She vaguely sensed Gavin pulling her to her feet, directing her hands beneath his shirt, and then she was lifting his shirt over his head. Her bare breasts dragged against the hair on his chest as he gathered her to him and guided her to the bed.

She lay back as he unfastened his falls and stepped out of his trousers. He was beautiful—lean and pale, with dark hair dusting his chest in a trail to his stomach, where his cock stood rigid. She stared, her throat dry.

"Christ, Emilia." Gavin's voice was rough. "Look at you. You've *ruined* me."

She opened her arms, and he came to her. Their frenetic pace slowed, the raging flames contained and simmering. She could feel him, impossibly hard against her stomach.

"You're not quite ruined yet," she managed to tease. "Almost."

She hooked her leg over his hip as she tentatively reached between them. She shivered, accepting she knew very little of this. Only what she'd learned from her own hand, from a secreted-away pamphlet, from the long ago gossip of girls at school. She would have to rely on Gavin for most of it.

They would have to rely on each other.

"Can I touch you?" she whispered.

"*Hell*," Gavin swore, his hand tightening at her hip. "Yes—yes, if you would like—"

She delicately ran her finger over his length, savoring the way his bliss frayed in his throat.

"How?" She watched his face.

"Just…" He closed his eyes and found her fingers, shaping them around his shaft. His entire body tensed as she curled her hand around the solid, silky weight of his cock, moving the way he showed her. "*Just* like that. God, Emilia—"

"Do you know…what to do?" She kissed his jaw, his mouth, his chin. "Because there cannot be a child. We must be…very cautious."

"I understand." His ears were red, but his eyes glittered. "I know that much."

She wound her arm around his neck, pulling him close enough to feel his heartbeat against her breast. "Then I'm ready."

"Yes?"

"*Yes.*"

She opened her legs, letting him settle, their hips pressing together.

His hand fell to his cock, and he slotted himself against her.

A pressure, a *sting*, mirrored in a sudden wet dewing her lashes.

The stretch was so heavy, so unexpected, her breath caught and she couldn't get it back.

Emilia gasped, tightly closing her eyes, shocked at the unyielding friction. She suddenly feared she would cry, and because it was Gavin, it would stop him, and she would lose this, the very thing she most wanted to keep.

She willed her body to relax, she willed herself to think of how good it felt to have his hand on her breast, how good it felt when his thumb circled her nipple.

"Emilia." Gavin's sigh came from her neck, his face pressed to her shoulder, and the foggy heat of his breath felt good too. She focused on that breath, on the tight exhale he brushed over her skin, the reminder he, too, was feeling *this* for the first time, and she woozily wondered if he liked it, if she was good for him.

"Emilia?" His voice was sharper, no longer in her shoulder. He was watching on her face how she struggled to take him. "Are you—"

"It will be fine," she panted, shifting her hips, trying to ease his entry, only making it worse. "It gets easier…I've heard it gets easier…it's just the first time—"

"You're not fine," he murmured, pushing onto his hands, looking over her in concern.

"I…I will be." She tried to clear her head. "Don't worry about me."

"No." His face fractured in dawning dismay. "*Shite*—you're not ready, Emilia."

Her heart cracked as he pulled back, relieving the pressure, and she ached twice over—in the tender spot between her legs and the tender spot behind her ribs, because it felt better to have him withdraw from her than enter her, and that surely couldn't be right.

She was all wrong, always, all the time.

"I'm ready," she whispered hoarsely. "Please. Gavin, I want this with you."

He lay back on the bed and rolled to his side, pulling her against him. His cock was still stiff, nudging hot into her hip.

"No, that's not what I meant," he murmured. He ran the back of his hand slowly, *slowly* between her breasts, down her stomach, all the way to her thatch of curls. She gasped as he stroked there, his thumb grazing her sex. Gavin watched her closely, his gaze as incendiary as the brush of his fingers. "I only meant, you aren't *ready*, sweetheart."

"Hmm?" She asked vaguely, spreading her legs wider, her eyelids growing heavy from his faint, maddening touch.

"I think we went too fast." He used his other hand to tuck back her hair, to tilt her chin to his. "Damn, if I'm not an idiot. I should have known better. This is what I feared. I'm so sorry, darling."

"*Oh*," she breathed, canting her hips toward the next slow sweep of his fingers. She felt a growing and exquisite glide and caught his meaning. "Yes. That's good, Gavin…"

She dragged her gaze to where he stroked her. The sight of his beautiful hand dipping between her splayed thighs elicited a sharp wave of pleasure, pulling resolutely toward her core. She gasped and arched her back, beckoning his touch in earnest.

"I believe I can fix this," he whispered, his eyes dark and intent as he braced himself above her. "If you'd like me to try."

"Yes." A blooming, eager rush volleyed against the raw ache, and she moaned a little. "But please, don't stop because of me."

"Shh." He kissed her ear. "Don't be foolish. I'll only start because of you."

Gavin moved slowly, forcing aside his own agonizing need. He wouldn't rush again. He was going to take his time, learn what she liked. Then and only then would he concede to giving himself over to pleasure.

He cupped her breast and she sighed…but no, *not enough*, not the shattering he sought. He caressed her, studying her. When he flicked her nipple, she loosened a throaty moan, and his blood sang with victory. He did it again, feathering his tongue over one taut peak, then the other, until Emilia grasped his hair. Her fingers tightened, and Gavin groaned with satisfaction.

"I'm sorry," she said raggedly. "I just…I need…"

"Yes," he muttered. To her, to himself. "Don't be sorry. You can tell me what you need."

"Ah…touch me again," she whispered tautly. "If you—"

He pressed his face to her stomach. "I know."

Somehow, he did know. He could see what she wanted in how she clenched and circled her hips. And he could give it to her. The sweet squirm of her body beneath him turned him mad and capable. Emilia was his to learn, so long as he paid attention.

He trailed his mouth to her hip.

"Gavin, *please...*"

He was fucking paying attention.

He brushed his lips up and down each spread leg. In the firelight she was all rose and gold—her damp and tangled hair, the tips of her nipples, the soft skin of her inner thighs.

He slid his hands beneath her, kneading the curve of her bottom, nudging her knees wider with his shoulders. He looked upon her for one more moment, coursing with nerves and ardor, then he opened his mouth against her sex, his tongue laving slow and soothing where moments ago he'd caused her ache.

"*Oh...*"

God—*yes.*

She was dampening under his tongue, her body growing pliant with desire. He could feel it on her slick folds; he could hear it in her jagged breath. If he pulled himself from the soft cradle of her thighs and looked at her face, he would see it there too—*there,* in the arch of her neck against the goose down pillow, *there* in the dusky shadow of her lowered lashes.

She was moaning indistinctly, her face pressing into her arm.

"Look at me, Emilia." She blinked slowly, but her unfocused gaze met his. "Is this better?"

If it wasn't, he'd never rest. He'd work her until they were both boneless. He needed to get this right, exactly right for her.

"Don't tell me it's fine," he warned, his chest tight. "You're not to appease me."

"I need...more," she admitted, lifting her hips to his mouth. "I need to *feel* you, Gavin."

Bloody hell. He dragged his tongue flat against her, opening her with a rough, insistent slide.

"Yes," she hissed. "Like that. *Yes.*"

He clenched his teeth so hard, his jaw burned in protest, but all he could hear were her rasping, precious words. *Yes. Yes.* Had he ever felt better than he did right now? He was emboldened by the potency of her need, by the understanding *he* could meet it.

Anything she wanted. Always.

"Hold your knees." He murmured the coarse command into her hip, too far gone to be surprised by the blunt force of his own words. He pressed his palms behind her thighs, finding no resistance as she grasped her own legs, blessedly holding herself open and apart for him. "Yes. Be good for me, Emilia."

"Is this…" Her question came from far away, ringing in his ears. "Gavin, I don't know—"

"It's perfect." He had nothing to compare this to, and he wasn't by nature a man indulgent with praise. But surely, the trail of her blush—starting at her throat, mapping his gaze across her body to the damp parting of her thighs—surely, this was perfection incarnate. "You're perfect, Emilia. You're perfectly right. You're perfect for me."

He slanted his tongue back against her sex, circling forcefully now. For once, the caustic saboteur inside his head was silenced by Emilia's husky moans. He concentrated with single-minded intent on the tilt of her hips, on the way she rocked herself against his mouth, on the way her fingernails dug into her own skin as she held her legs open for him.

She cried out, and his cock pulsed against the bed linens. He was rapidly losing hold of the situation. Beneath him, she was gradually, undeniably tensing, and he sensed that what he'd been trying to build was about to crest.

"Emilia." His breath moved over her quim. *So sensitive. So close.* "Can you let go?"

"I want to…" Her back arched on the bed. "But I can't possibly…end this."

Gavin groaned in acknowledgment. She wanted to stay here,

strung out in the golden gleaming in-between, fulfilled and yearning, the two halves completing her.

He wanted it too.

But he couldn't stop, because this was its own kind of intoxication. Every swipe of his tongue tipped her closer to the edge, until she was faintly begging for it, until he relented and gave it to her. When he finally pushed one finger inside her, she nearly wept with the force of her release.

She convulsed around his hand, and he kissed her thighs, scarcely able to believe he'd wrung this pleasure from her. Her shoulders lifted sharply before slackening against the mattress as she covered her face, gasping. Her gilded hair spilled across her shoulders, over the tips of her breasts.

"Gavin…"

"Perfect," he repeated huskily, beholding her as she came back to him. "You're so damn perfect, Emilia."

"Now…" She smiled, breathless and radiant. "*Now* I'm ready to ruin you."

He puffed a laugh, but he could no longer deny his own arousal. With a grunt, he moved back up her body. This time, when he pressed his tip against her sex, she yielded to him. He quaked at the sublime slide and fought to master the sensation of just how unbearably good it felt to work himself inside her.

"Slower." She exhaled shakily. "If you can…"

He willed himself to comply, resisting the urge to take her to the hilt. His blood was racing, his heart beating in his cock. Instincts he had long denied sharpened his senses, directing him to drive, to claim, to take what she offered. He sank deeper, stretching her.

"Emilia…" He brushed back her damp hair. "Sweetheart. I…I need to push."

"Yes." She gripped his biceps. "But kiss me."

He slid his hand to her throat, tilting her face, kissing her hard. Two quick, deep thrusts saw him fully seated within her. His bollocks swayed against the soft curve of her bottom and his vision clouded. He was nearly out of his mind.

"Breathe," he murmured, stroking her bottom lip with his thumb. "Breathe."

Emilia sucked in a rattling gasp, but her heel notched behind his thigh, pulling him closer. She clung to him, and he let her, holding steady until he felt her tension ease.

"There," she whispered. She opened her eyes, the amber blurring to black. "It's *good*." She rolled her hips, testing, and his resolve almost fractured. "You can take me, Gavin."

Take me.

Everything he'd asked of her, she'd given him—her words, her body. He wouldn't diminish her by asking again, by keeping them in this purgatory of half measures. Finally, he let himself move, he gave her his control. He was drowning, the wet heat of her enveloping him, around him, below him. Her flaxen hair was in his hands and against his forehead; her skin was dewy and flushed. Everywhere he put his mouth was as sweet and soft as the gasps in his ear.

"Can I...harder—" He was unraveling. He had no idea what he was asking.

"Yes." She fisted his hair, holding his face to hers. There was an abyss widening inside him, echoing from Emilia's luminous gaze back to his own chest. "Let go."

He held her legs apart, his shoulders bowing under the weight of need—wild, carnal, overwhelming. *Faster. Deeper.* He was through with withholding, and Emilia accepted it all. She was a dream. His dream. *His.*

Gavin raked his gaze over the perspiration dotting her neck, the rapid rise and fall of her breasts, her slack, rosy lips. She was so beautiful, it hurt. He wished he could last longer for her, but his cock surged, the familiar tingle building at the base of his spine.

"I'm going to come," he groaned, his pleasure constricting in regret. "I can't wait—"

"Good," she murmured into his neck. "Don't wait. You already attended to me. I want this for *you*."

With a grunt, he withdrew from her, kneeling and fisting his cock. Emilia reached for him, stroking his stomach until he shuddered, the force of his climax hurtling toward him. He pulled her close, kissing her deeply as he spent between them.

He looked down at her, breathing hard.

"Bloody *hell*, Emilia."

She burst into exhilarated laughter, and he joined her. He felt thoroughly dismantled. It was a damn wonder.

"My God." She cupped his cheeks. "Gavin. *Diligent* was only half of it."

He turned her hand and kissed her wrist. Reluctantly, he climbed from the bed and staggered to the copper tub, finding a cloth and dipping it in the now-tepid bathwater.

"Oh, you don't need to bother," she protested, sitting up. "I can manage—"

Gavin ignored her and brought her the cloth, stirred by how she looked in his bed. Emilia was beaming but shivering, as though the rush had finally caught up to her.

"The paltriest of offerings." He smiled sheepishly as he drew the cloth over her stomach and between her legs. "The bath grew cold."

"Not paltry." She watched his hands slide tenderly over her. "Not in the least."

He eased her back against the pillows and wrapped his arm around her, cocooning her beneath the counterpane.

"Warm now?" he murmured into her shoulder.

"Yes." She stroked his forearm, her fingernails a gentle score along his skin. "I'm warm now."

For an interminable stretch of time, he traced aimless patterns up and down her shoulder blades, and she was so quiet, he thought she must have fallen asleep.

"The snow," she murmured drowsily, drawing him from his musings. "Did it stop?"

The curtains of his four-poster were drawn back, and he raised his head to look out the window. "Yes," he whispered. "Nothing to worry about. It didn't even stick."

"Hmm." She rolled over in his arms, pressing her face to his chest. "But wouldn't it have been lovely if it had?"

12

EMILIA WOKE in the cold blue dawn of Christmas morning wrapped in warmth. Gavin's bedsheets were piled around her, the drawn bedcurtains keeping her shadowed and snug. She stretched, sighing at the pleasing, dull ache in her arms and between her thighs.

She rolled over and noticed she was alone. Heaven only knew where Gavin had gone so early on Christmas Day. He was probably doing something energetic and austere, like a snowy dawn hike or correcting Leo's map of Sparta. She curled into his pillow, inhaling his scent—soap and ink and sweat.

Gavin.

Her whole body blushed with recollection. She was happy, *so happy*. Last night, she had felt so tenderly beloved. It seemed as if a great secret had been unlocked for her, as if she would never be the same again.

How could she be? Surely, her life was irrevocably changed.

She curled beneath the blankets, thinking it over. The notion was startling, but undeniable: she likely couldn't work as a governess anymore. Thomas the groom had seen Gavin take her upstairs last night. He might have told others in the household by now. It was inevitable the Traverses would find out.

But it didn't frighten her anymore.

Ever since the inn, something had unfurled between her and Gavin, gathering and growing, planting itself in her dreams, twining around her intentions. And last night, it had covered over her completely. It was rather intoxicating to see a mild-mannered man lose his mind. It made a woman act foolishly and hope dangerously.

But in the light of day, it didn't feel foolish or dangerous. For once, Emilia's daydreams drifted not so very far above her. A future where she wasn't a governess but Gavin's *wife*. Her dream house, no longer imaginary.

She had never thought it possible.

Would she miss her work? Yes, some of it. The children, the creativity, the sense of purpose. But there was so much she wouldn't miss. The crippling loneliness. The oppressive insecurity. The sorrow over never having a family of her own.

She would miss the work, but she wouldn't miss the life.

Not if she was embarking on a new one.

There was a light knock at the door, and Emilia jumped. She hastily wrapped herself in Gavin's dressing gown.

"It's me," he murmured, and her startle shifted to a smile. She eased open the door, finding him pink-cheeked with his coat thrown over his shoulders.

"You don't have to knock on your own door," she teased, letting him inside. "It's *your* bedchamber."

Her greeting was a bit muffled, seeing as Gavin was already kissing her, as slowly as he had the first time at the inn. And then he groaned and pinned her to the door, kissing her as relentlessly as he had last night.

Emilia sighed against his mouth. A perfect good night kiss was even better in the morning.

"Merry Christmas," he finally whispered. "That's the first thing I need to tell you."

"Merry Christmas." She beamed.

He pulled her close, following the stretch of her smile, brushing his lips over the curve of her cheek.

"The second thing you need to tell me?"

"I can't remember." He nuzzled her neck. "Your dimple wreaks havoc on me."

"I have a present for you." She scraped her fingers through his hair until the thick waves were gorgeously mussed. She loved being the only one to see him like this.

"Yes, please." He teased the opening of the dressing gown and Emilia yelped, swatting away his frigid hands.

"Are you a cad now? *I'm* not the present." She laughed, glowing from within. What a wonder, a man with cold fingers, kissing her on Christmas. "Your hands are like ice. Where were you?"

"I was in the stables," Gavin muttered, looking her over. "Is this my dressing gown?"

"I'm hoping to abscond with it." She casually lifted her shoulder, letting the neckline gape wider. "It's wonderfully cozy."

"Yes, well. That certainly won't assuage the concerns of Thomas, who I fear has vilified me," Gavin said distractedly, staring at the shadowed curve of her breast. "I'm out trying to cover our tracks, and you're marching about in a state of undress."

Emilia took him in—hair flopping, eyes bright, cheeks flushed. He looked like a boy who wanted to be teased by a girl, and she felt like the kind of girl who could do it. Leaning forward, she placed her hands on his chest, on his waistcoat, where he kept his spectacles. She nimbly snaked her hand inside the pocket, finding the spectacles and slipping them over her nose.

"Who could ever think *you* a villain?" She grinned mischievously, lowering her voice in an approximation of Gavin's. "For my first dastardly deed, I'll bring my legal briefs to a

Christmas party. And *then* I'll shock women and children by drawing maps of Sparta to scale—"

She had no sense of depth perception with the magnified lenses of the spectacles, which meant she was entirely unprepared for the bruising force of his kiss.

"God—" His voice fell. "What are you *doing* to me, Emilia?"

He yanked her against him, and she moaned. He was hard, *so hard* already, and it did wicked and wonderful things to her belly. His palms smoothed over her shoulders, pushing open the dressing gown to bare her breasts.

"You can keep the spectacles," he muttered against her throat. "You'll have to. I'm going to think of you like this every time I see them."

"You're out of your mind." Emilia laughed as his chilly fingertips trailed along the small of her back. "What's gotten into you today?"

"You." His voice was like gravel as he palmed her buttocks. "*You*. In my bed. In my clothing. In my goddamned spectacles. You've upended me, Emilia."

She gasped and parted her legs. "You've upended me, as well," she breathed unevenly. Had she been teasing him only a moment ago? "It's not only you, Gavin."

"No, it *won't* be only me." His expression was hot and unfocused. "Put your hand with mine." His lips brushed hers, opening her mouth. "Let's find out how you like it first thing in the morning."

She closed her eyes, shivering as she slid her hand down his forearm, meeting his fingers where they teased her sex. His hand was alongside hers, the pads of his fingers searching, then sure, and much larger than her own. He ground his finger against her bud, and she was melting, desire pooling hot and shocking, and he found it, he used it, rubbing slick and hard where she was nothing but sensation. He groaned quietly, and the slivered fracture of Gavin's composure only sharpened her pleasure.

"What are you thinking?" she managed. She grasped his wrist, holding him against her.

"I'm thinking…you like it slow." His voice was low and thick in her ear as his finger curled inside her. "You like when I draw… it…out." He did just so, and her sinking moan proved him right. Gavin's face grew slack. "I'm thinking I like it slow too."

He flattened his tongue to her painfully hard nipple, and Emilia cried out, so good did it feel. She *did* like it slow, with his hazy concentration on her face.

But she also liked it fast, like last night, when his neck curved to her collarbone and his shoulders flexed and she was lost in the searing force of his claim. This was Gavin, and he was hers, and she would like it anyway they discovered it together.

"Gavin…"

"Can I give you more?" He dropped to his knees, staring up at her with that familiar, beseeching resolve.

"You can always give me more," she whispered, and her assurance seemed to fuel him. Gavin had worried he couldn't care for her, but his care was her undoing. His mouth and hands followed every shaky sigh, every desperate twist of her hips, until he was pitching her right against her peak. At the shudder tearing down her spine, a small smirk of victory teased the corner of his lips, and Emilia's vision blurred.

But it had nothing to do with spectacles.

AFTER, when they were winded and sated, Emilia sat with Gavin's head in her lap. She hummed absently, rubbing the hard knots in his temples. Holding him this way was an altogether different sort of gratification.

"Do you always have such tension here?" She worked her fingers in steady, soothing strokes, down his forehead.

"Yes." He groaned softly. "Always."

"What was the second thing you needed to tell me?"

"Hmm?"

"You told me the first thing you needed to say was *Merry Christmas*. What was the second thing?"

"Oh." He sat up, reaching for her hand. "Just that you needn't worry. I spoke to Thomas. That's why I was at the stables at dawn."

"You spoke to Thomas?" She cocked her head. "At *dawn*?"

"He won't tell anyone what happened." Gavin brushed back her hair. "Nobody knows...well, except Nate. Thomas did speak with him last night. But nobody else. And I can handle Nate." He paused, considering. "Or at least, I'll figure out how to handle him."

Emilia stared at him, her heart slipping a bit sideways.

Nobody knows.

Gavin had ensured their secret was safe.

Emilia wasn't certain she *wanted* to keep it a secret.

But Gavin had gone to the trouble—in the freezing dawn of Christmas Day—and she could now see that his caution made sense. What bloomed between them was new. They should nurture it away from the rest of the world.

Surely, it was for the best.

"Emilia? Is everything all right?"

She decided to change the subject. All her wishing had left her a bit wobbly, and she could benefit from something useful...like an agenda.

"What will Christmas Day be like?"

"Cora insists on church for Christmas—should be a madhouse with Oliver and Tess—and then presents for the children. Dinner will be early so the servants can have the evening off and begin their holiday. It's all fairly relaxed." He grimaced. "I need to work a bit this afternoon, though."

"On Christmas?" She frowned. "Is it the brief you told me about yesterday?"

"It is." Gavin sighed. "I need to write to the client."

"What is the case about?"

He looked at her in surprise. "You'd like to hear about it?"

"Of course." Emilia stroked her finger between his eyebrows. "It's got you making a face. I can tell it's weighing on you…" She hesitated. "Perhaps I could help?"

"Yes…" he said slowly. "You could, actually. I would appreciate your insight. I didn't want to bother you. It's a bit complicated."

"It's no bother." She shook her head. "Go on, tell me about it."

Gavin climbed to his feet and went over to his table to sort through some papers. He returned with a small pile of newspaper clippings arranged in chronological order.

Emilia flipped through the documents, her heart first sinking, then nearly breaking.

"Charity Matthews is a governess," she said softly, looking up at Gavin. "She was engaged to this young man?"

"Yes."

"And he ended the betrothal…"

She stared at the papers, reluctantly imagining what it would be like to have a whole new future dangled in front of her then ripped away.

"She's suing him, as is her right." Gavin rubbed his hands over his face. "And he's seeking defense counsel, as is *his* right."

"What happens if she wins?" Emilia thumbed gently over the clippings, thinking of Charity Matthews, who would likely never again be able to stomach reading a newspaper after this rot.

"She'll be awarded a sum. Reparations, for her trouble." Gavin frowned. "And, to your forthcoming question, if Samuel Norwood wins, she'll get nothing."

Nothing.

"She already has nothing." Emilia's vision swam with empathetic tears. "She'll *never* work again. My God. I can't imagine how frightened she is. She must feel deeply swindled by this young man, to go to all this trouble." She looked at Gavin, piecing together what he'd told her yesterday. The door he was loath to walk through. "What will you do? If you agree to be Mr. Norwood's defense counsel, you'll be offered the opportunity to advance?"

"Yes," he said, resigned. "That's the crux of it. If I agree to plead for him, his father will put in a good word for me, I'll likely be made serjeant, and my first brief will be this one. And damn it, I *know* how it sounds. It's morally reprehensible."

He did seem to know how it sounded; he looked positively miserable. Even still, for the sake of Charity Matthews, Emilia felt compelled to confirm it.

"That it is." She handed him the papers, wanting to distance herself from them. "It is most certainly morally reprehensible. Gavin, what they are proposing you do…" She trailed off, unable to consider it.

Gavin hung his head. "I'm going mad, Emilia, trying to foresee every possible conclusion. I need to look beyond this single case. But I feel so *useless*—"

His disquiet was painful to witness.

"Stop." Emilia pressed a finger to his mouth. "Stop talking that way. You are *not* useless. I want you to remember that. I fully believe you already know what to do, Gavin. There is a clear choice here."

"What would you do?" He was staring hard at her. "If it were you in Miss Matthews's position?"

"Goodness." Emilia had heard of these situations before, but it was impossible to imagine. "I…don't know that I'd be brave enough to do anything. For decades, I haven't had anywhere to call my own. It's been so constant, I sometimes forget it could be *worse*. I always have at least the *promise* of future employment." She shook her head. "Miss Matthews…after this scandal, she won't even have that."

"I wish you'd had a different life, Emilia," Gavin said quietly. "I wish it hadn't been so hard for you." He kissed her knuckles. "If I could alter any circumstances, they would be yours."

Emilia stilled, stroking his beautiful dark hair. She loved his curls, and wished he didn't comb over them. She loved his face. She loved his hesitant smile and his twilight eyes and the tense bunches of muscles where he held all his cares.

She loved *him*.

"My circumstances are perfect, Gavin." She cradled his cheek. "Today, they are perfect."

"THERE YOU ARE, SINCLAIR." Nate's voice drifted from the threshold of the library. "If I didn't know better, I'd think you were avoiding me."

It was midafternoon on Christmas Day, and Gavin had, assuredly, been avoiding Nate. Needless to say, between church, presents, and Tess's rather aggressive musical performance, Gavin had endured his brother-in-law's questioning glances but, fortunately, no questions.

But now Nate had found him.

"Right." Nate strode into the library. He crossed his arms and appraised Gavin. "Do you have anything you want to tell me?"

"No," Gavin muttered, returning to the letter he was writing. "I do not."

Nate narrowed his eyes. "Do you have anything you *need* to tell me?"

"Yes." Gavin turned over the parchment, beginning a new line of correspondence. "You'll need to hire a new governess."

"Sinclair."

Gavin ignored him.

"I advised you to take Miss Davis Christmas shopping. That was the plan yesterday. For you to escort her to town."

"Yes," Gavin allowed. "Your recollection is accurate. I did, indeed, escort her to the shops."

Nate raised his eyebrow. "What in hell sort of present did you give her?"

Gavin sighed and set down his quill. "Is Cora upset?"

"Cora does not yet know." Nate speared him with a look. "Consider this my gift to you. My aim is for my wife to have a lovely Christmas, so I haven't told her what Thomas told *me* upon my return last night."

"Right." Gavin reddened and cleared his throat. "What, precisely, did Thomas tell you?"

He assumed Thomas's report had something to do with Gavin hauling the lovely, earnest new governess to his chambers to ostensibly—and accurately—ravish her. *She ravished me too*, he wanted to say. *And she will again. I intend to marry her.* But that didn't seem like the sort of thing a man announced first to his brother-in-law.

When he woke that morning, Gavin's priority had been to spare Emilia the scrutiny of Nate and Cora's household. He didn't want to make assumptions, to force her hand. What happened between them couldn't be yet another set of circumstances foisted upon her. He wanted their future to be her choice. He wanted to give her the space and clarity to make it.

"Thankfully, no details." Nate raised his hands, shaking his head. His good humor slowly dissipated, his face growing serious. "But, Sinclair, I am Miss Davis's employer. I'm responsible for safeguarding her wellbeing and reputation. You do know, I hope, that if anything has *progressed* between you, you need to right that ship. Immediately."

Gavin stared at him. It was always a bit of a shock when easygoing Nate turned grave. It sometimes seemed as though he had no business being stern and running a household. But he did. An entire family depended on him, and he was gladly accountable. This was Nate's life now.

Men changed.

Gavin was changing.

"Travers." Gavin paused, judiciously choosing his words. "It's no idle dalliance on my part. Though I must ask for your discretion for the time being. It's new—painfully new—but rest assured, I'll speak to her."

"See that you do." Nate held his frown for a beat longer, then relaxed. "Now. Allow me to be the first to congratulate you, Sinclair."

"For what?" Gavin's ears were turning pink.

"For taking my advice." Nate grinned as he headed for the door. "If there's one thing I know, it's how to woo a woman at Aldworth Park."

Gavin watched him depart, caught between mortification and pride. He *had* wooed a woman, hadn't he? By some miracle, reserved Gavin Sinclair had managed to win the girl.

And he intended to do right by her.

He exhaled and returned his attention to his correspondence. He reread the note, shoring up his nerves.

Norwood: I believe further communication between us would benefit from a conversation. Seeing as you and I are in the same vicinity over Christmas, my sister will send an invitation for dinner this week. I would like to conclude our business prior to the new year.

There. What's done is done.

For the first time, Gavin didn't feel an abject sense of dread about this brief. His talk with Emilia had convinced him, solving his conundrum in one fell swoop.

Although it wasn't really a *swoop*.

It was an unbounded plummet.

Gavin was falling for her. Ardently, undeniably, actively falling for her. And he never wanted to land. It was tremendously frightening and fantastically thrilling. He felt as though the entire world was right side up, and he'd only now discovered it was wrong before.

He knew what he needed to do, whether he liked it or not.

This wasn't about his ethics or his character; the entire quandary now seemed wretchedly selfish.

He'd failed someone he loved once before. He wouldn't do it again.

There was a woman who needed him.

And she was waiting for him upstairs.

13

———————

Christmas dinner was a chaotic affair, made more so by the arrival of the Christmas pudding.

"Papa, listen. Tess will pour the sauce, and I'll light the spill." Leo stood on his chair, surveying the proceedings. "We arranged it already."

"Oh, did you?" Mr. Travers cocked his head. "You two will oversee brandy and flames? I'm so relieved. It might otherwise go badly."

"To be clear." Mrs. Travers squeezed her husband's forearm. "Your father will manage the pudding."

"It's our turn." Tess's cheeks reddened. Emilia had noted the little girl was remarkably strong in her convictions regarding equity. "We never get to do it, not for *one* Christmas—"

"When you are taller than your mother, you can do the pudding." Mr. Travers winked. "So next year for Leo."

Emilia let the bedlam wash over her. She was stuffed full of venison and drowsy from wine and her thoroughly sleepless night with Gavin. As if reading her mind from across the table, he caught her gaze and held it. She let him; it felt lovely to be regarded by someone you loved in a room full of people.

Mr. Travers poured the brandy and set the Christmas pudding ablaze. Oliver hollered in delight, then lost his temper when he learned the trick couldn't be repeated.

"Do we need to watch out for silver?" Gavin asked, poking at his pudding. He looked around the table. Everyone was laughing or squabbling or ensuring portions were even. He looked at Emilia and shrugged ruefully.

She thrummed with fondness. He would rather break his teeth than cause an interruption. "Mrs. Travers," she called loudly. "Are there sixpence in the pudding?"

"Oh." Mrs. Travers glanced up. "No. Between the choking and the tears over not getting one, we can't reasonably carry on that particular tradition."

"We've decided it's best we lose together rather than win alone." Mr. Travers grinned at his wife. "Sound logic, don't you think?"

"It seems perfectly reasonable to me." Emilia chanced a smile at Gavin. "But sometimes, everyone wins."

It was late when Gavin finally made his way to Emilia's room. He knocked lightly, fearing she was already asleep, but she opened the door at once. Candlelight danced over her soft white night rail and her plait of flaxen hair.

"I'm sorry. I had to wait until Nate and Cora retired," he murmured. "I didn't want to take any chances tonight."

"I'm glad you're here." Her dimple beckoned him inside. "I'd just been thinking I never gave you your present. I meant to give this to you earlier." She wrinkled her nose. "Though be warned, it's not very exciting."

She guided him to the wingback chair next to the fire and handed him a small parcel. Gavin unwound the paper, half fearing it would be a peppermint stick. His blood heated at the memory.

Come to think of it, a peppermint might have distinct advantages right now.

"It's a quill pen," Emilia blurted before he finished opening it. "Because you broke two this week." She had the decency to look charmingly guilty. "It seemed the least I could do."

"The *least* you could do was end my torment." He smoothed his palm up her back and kissed her bottom lip, dragging it gently between his teeth until she hummed. "Which, thankfully, you did."

"Now who's tormenting?" Her eyes gleamed playfully as she plucked the quill away. "Truly, you don't need to keep it. I can now see this is a very poor present—"

Gavin lifted the goose feather quill from her fingers and held it in the firelight. The pen was untreated and durable with a well-cut nib.

"Hush." He leveled the quill at her, the feather just touching her lip. "That's nonsense. This is an excellent pen."

She blushed beautifully, and he pulled her into his lap.

"I thought you might use it to write," she pointed out helpfully.

"A logical assumption."

"No." She swatted his shoulder. "I meant...you might use it to write to *me*." She swallowed, growing contemplative. "After you return to London."

Gavin furrowed his brow. "Why would I need to write to you when I'm in London?"

"Oh." Her face grew pale. "I didn't...of course. Of course you don't need to. I don't expect that. I shouldn't have assumed..."

She looked down, her lashes dark against her cheek.

"Emilia." He edged her closer, kissing her frown. "No. I only mean I won't need to write to you from London because I very much hope you will be there *with* me."

"You do?" Her arms tightened around him. "You shouldn't say it if it's not true."

Gavin recalled what she told him yesterday, how she hadn't

been certain he wanted her. He had to remember, always, that this beautifully resilient woman was woven with insecurities. The thoughtless disregard of others was imprinted beneath her skin.

He needed to be brave and direct with her because she deserved it.

"Emilia…" He tilted her chin. "The ease I feel with you…it's rare for me. *All* of this is rare. I'm not bold. I'm not a man who takes. But I'm not a man who lets go either. And I'm not letting go of you when I return to London."

Her eyes were very bright. He savored the flickering russet in her gaze; never had he been regarded with such exquisite clarity. From the moment he met her, Gavin had been perfectly, imperfectly himself. And it felt so damn *good*.

"I feel the same," she murmured, and his chest expanded in relief. "Just the same. But it seems frightening to admit." She shrugged helplessly, her night rail slipping down her shoulder. "What's between us…it's still so new."

"It is," he acknowledged, brushing his mouth over hers. "It is new." He toyed with the edge of her night rail. "Would it be all right with you, if we didn't keep it that way?"

"Yes." She tunneled her hands into his hair and beamed impishly. "Let's watch it get very old. In fact, let's *tarnish* it."

He groaned against the sweet press of her lips, splaying one hand at her nape and unwinding her braid. Then it was only warm breath finding warm skin. Clothing fell away, and she pulled him to her bed in a tangle of searching kisses and wandering hands.

"Roll to your stomach," he murmured, and Emilia complied, spreading her legs as he swept up her hair. He gently turned her face toward the bedside chest so she could see the quill she'd given him, the quill he would never use to write a letter to her.

"I'm keeping it." He lowered his mouth to her ear. "All of it. I'm keeping everything."

He trailed his hand down the base of her spine. She was dimpled here, too—two captivating crescents stamped above the curve of her bottom, summoning his hands and mouth. He teased her, drawing his fingers along the slick softness between her thighs. Slowly, he thumbed her wet sex, lightly circling until she moaned, until she lifted her hips, until she reached back for him. Her hand found his aching cock and guided him, hard and heavy, inside her.

He loved holding her like this, half-draped over her, kissing her mouth and eyelids as he thrust slowly, patiently, finding his pace. She came first in a gradual wave, keening into the pillow, taking him with her, right to where they both belonged.

Emilia spent the morning of St. Stephen's Day working on Leo's handwriting; somewhere along the way he'd developed an awkward grip. She wasn't certain how long she was to remain his governess, but she was still his governess today. Improving his penmanship seemed the least she could do.

"Pinch just here." She angled the slate pencil in his small hand. "Good. Doesn't that feel better on your wrist?"

Leo frowned at the lines she set him. "Ten? Will that be enough practice?"

"Plenty for the day after Christmas," she assured him.

Emilia smiled fondly as he bit his lip and got to work. Leaving him to concentrate, she drifted across the parlor. Mrs. Travers was organizing donations for the servants and looked as though she could use some assistance.

"Will Mr. Travers participate in the hunt today?" Emilia asked, handing over a stack of folded scarves. She'd heard mention of another party hosted by some friends.

"Lord and Lady Monmouth invited us, so yes, we'll go." Mrs. Travers shook her head. "In truth, we aren't usually so busy. We prefer to just be here. At home." She smiled.

Emilia knew it was dreadfully suspicious of her to ask, but she couldn't help it. "And…Mr. Sinclair? Will he likewise attend the hunt?"

She kept her voice very light. Possibly too light. Mrs. Travers tilted her head, her eyes flickering in inquiry, but then she turned her attention to boxing up a set of teacups.

"No, my brother isn't going. He said he has some work to do." Mrs. Travers deflated slightly. "Again."

"I see," Emilia acknowledged.

"You know…" Mrs. Travers shook her head. "I really thought the worst of it would be over with the resolution of my guardianship dispute."

"Did he help you with it?" Emilia was blatantly overstepping, but Mrs. Travers seemed too contemplative to notice.

"Help? Heavens, he worked himself to the bone trying to correct course for me." She smiled sadly.

"He did?" Emilia's heart clenched.

"It's nearly *all* he did for a long time. Gavin was a godsend. I would have fallen to pieces without him." Mrs. Travers sighed. "I only wish he would give himself a bit of grace. He works so hard, all the time, even over the holidays."

"Yes," Emilia said, because it seemed a safe response. She didn't want to tell Mrs. Travers she was well aware of how hard Gavin worked.

"He even invited a colleague to dinner this week," Mrs. Travers went on. "I don't mind, of course, but he won't even *consider* taking a few days off. He was adamant about hosting the Norwood family. Actually, Miss Davis, it would be lovely if you could join us, because then I'll have an even number, if you feel agreeable to hearing legalese over four courses."

Emilia could only stare at her.

"Did you say…Norwood?" She finally asked. "Mr. Sinclair invited the Norwoods to come to dinner?"

"Yes. Apparently, he's one of the men who can recommend

Gavin for his promotion. I'll have to be clever with the menu. I want to impress, you know, but also be welcoming."

"I'm sure you'll think of something marvelous, Mrs. Travers." Emilia's head was starting to ache. "Ah. If you'll excuse me, I'm feeling a bit peculiar."

"It's likely due to the Christmas pudding." Mrs. Travers shook her head. "Nate completely overdid it with the brandy."

"I'll be back, Leo," Emilia called. "Just keep practicing, please."

Emilia made her way upstairs, a faintly queasy feeling overtaking her. *Why would the Norwoods be coming for dinner?* If Gavin was declining the case in favor of the governess, he would just write to the Norwoods' solicitor...wouldn't he? He certainly wouldn't have his sister go to the trouble of hosting them.

She wasn't entirely sure it was her place to ask these questions...but yes. *Yes,* it was. Only yesterday, she had held him and seen the way he tormented himself, and she did not, she *did not* understand what he was thinking.

Her fist rapped his door more sharply than she'd intended, and Emilia stared at her hand, almost surprised by the force of her knock.

"Hello there." Gavin took her hand and pulled her inside.

She looked him over; gone was yesterday's sweet dishevelment. He was back to combed hair and neat cuffs.

And now Emilia felt a bit messy.

"How are you—"

"Gavin," she interrupted, not having the stomach nor temperament to play coy. "Why did your sister just tell me Mr. and Mrs. Norwood are coming for dinner this week?" She marched into his room. "Is that the way you tell a client you *aren't* taking their case?"

Gavin slowly shut his door and turned to face her. His expression was grave. "Emilia."

"Please don't tell me—"

"I'm taking the brief." His jaw twitched, but she didn't think it was hiding a smile this time. "I've written to Norwood, and he's coming to dinner so we can discuss the details. In particular, a revised stratagem. This gossip about Miss Matthews must stop—"

She stared at him, a wash of gray sinking through her. She recognized the uneasy melancholy for what it was: disappointment. She was *disappointed* in Gavin Sinclair. She couldn't believe this, after what they'd talked about, after what she'd told him.

"You're taking the brief."

"Yes. I am."

"You're going to defend Samuel Norwood against a woman trying to salvage herself from ruin?"

"Yes."

To his credit, he did not look away from her. He was calm and straight-shouldered and very, very steady…which was, perhaps, the worst part of all.

"Gavin." She pressed her hands over her eyes. "Why would you do this?"

Emilia had been let down before. She had yet to cast off the dismay she felt in Mrs. Granger's offensively green parlor, when her employment was unexpectedly terminated. But this was different. Gavin held himself to impossibly high standards. It hadn't even *occurred* to her that he wouldn't meet his own criteria for decency, that he wouldn't leap clear over it.

He was a deeply kind and honorable man, and Emilia had been ready to put her entire future in his tender hands.

Please be who I thought you were.

Her eyes were still squeezed shut, but she heard him cross the room, stopping right in front of her. She felt his hand come to her cheek, then lightly touch her hair.

"Because I want to take care with you."

"*What?*" She lowered her hands, staring at him in shock. That was the last possible answer she'd expected. "What on earth are you talking about?"

Gavin's brow furrowed. "I was thinking of you. Of your life. Of the life I want to give you. If we..." He trailed off, running his hand nervously through his hair.

Good. He should be nervous. He was making deranged choices, and she was going to hold him accountable for them.

But then he slotted his palm against hers, lacing their fingers together. She stared at their clasped hands. She had a vague sense that everything she most wanted was coming at a terrible price.

"You've never even had a ribbon, Emilia."

"Then buy me a ribbon." She dropped his hand and pinched the bridge of her nose. "Don't buy my future at the cost of your character."

He exhaled, rubbing his neck.

"Gavin." She once again clutched his hand. "If you want to please me, *think* of me. I'm a *governess*. Miss Matthews could have been me." She looked away as she voiced the terrifying truth. "It *could* be me. We aren't..."

"We aren't what?" His hand spasmed in hers. "What aren't we, Emilia?"

"You want to keep it a secret," she whispered. "What's happening between us. You don't want anyone to know." She took a deep breath. "And maybe that's for the best. Maybe this was meant to be like the inn, fleeting and freeing and—"

"No," Gavin interjected. "No. We aren't doing that."

He cupped her cheek. His gaze was warm and intense, and she once again let it capture her. She stepped nearer, and he pressed his forehead to hers.

"I kept our relationship quiet because it was prudent to do so until we wrapped our minds around it. I meant what I told you last night. Emilia, I'm in this with you. Are you in it with me? Because this is the nature of my work. This is my real life. I sometimes have to set my own feelings aside in order to do what's best in the long run."

"The *long run*?" She shook her head, trying to hold tears at bay.

"I don't want security at the expense of someone else. I don't want to belong somewhere so badly as that."

"Fine." He crossed his arms, his jaw tight. "Fine. Put yourself aside. Never mind the fact that if we marry, you can no longer be hired as a governess. Never mind the fact that if I snub my nose at someone as powerful as Norwood, I'll be lucky if I'm *ever* given a brief again. Never mind that we'll need to *make a living* if we want to live. Put *all of those* logistical concerns aside and pretend they don't matter."

She winced. "Gavin—"

"What about the next Miss Matthews?" He ticked off his fingers. "What about the next woman who finds herself on the cusp of financial ruin because of the fickle decision of a man? What about the next woman who wants to easily—or even feasibly— leave her marriage?" His voice cracked. "What about the next woman who wants to keep bloody custody of *her own bloody children*?" He was breathing hard. "What about them, Emilia? If I don't work my way to a position of power, I cannot change anything. I cannot *fix* anything."

Emilia's eyes burned, finally understanding the scope of his anguish. He was so *conflicted*. For how long? How long had he been driving himself forward in this way, carrying guilt she didn't understand?

"You told me you admire the way I move through life," she murmured. "Do you know how I do that? I've learned to make the best of it. I try to do my best—where I can, when I can."

He sank to his chair, his head bowed. Emilia came to him, and he pressed his face against her thigh.

"I understand you cannot abide me if I don't defend this poor woman. But can't you see?" His voice was hoarse. "I cannot abide myself if I don't try to stop there being so many women who need defending."

"Gavin." Emilia's cheeks were wet. "You did help your sister.

She told me. And, my love, sometimes one is enough. You can start with *one*."

She could see why he thought this way, so ordered, so rational. But she wanted more from him. She wanted more *for* him. She wanted him to put his plan and his guilt aside.

But she couldn't make him do it alone.

"I don't agree with you taking this case," she said slowly, her fingers soothing along his nape. "I don't like it…at all."

"I know. Nor do I." He looked up at her. "But can you be there for me anyway?"

She touched his mouth, feeling deeply uneasy. Gavin wasn't acting cruelly on purpose. And he was right on one point—the charm of the inn, the enchantment of Aldworth Park, they had to be left behind. These weren't the places where she and Gavin would build their life.

Their house would be real, in the real world.

"Yes," she finally said. "I can be there for you."

She gently touched his chin with her little finger.

"Thank you," he murmured.

For a long time, they embraced in silence, her arms around his shoulders, his face against her stomach.

And Emilia tried not to think of Charity Matthews, who threw her life away for something as fragile as a promise.

14

———————

The Norwoods wrote to accept Cora's invitation for the evening of December 29, and Gavin was back to his old habits—not sleeping and overthinking.

Over the last three days, he and Emilia had fallen into an uneasy accord. She still came to his bed and they made love, taking each other apart, holding each other together. They still lay awake, talking late into the night, but never about Gavin's choices, which hung heavily between them. Her silent censure was penance for the unsavory business he was about to engage in.

He was glad for her condemnation. He deserved it.

Nevertheless, she fell asleep holding his hand, tucking her feet against his while he stared at the canopy and sifted his fingers through her hair, making her wordless promises. At the end of the day, she *trusted* him, and there was nothing more important or simple than that. Emilia—who never asked anyone for anything— was asking he do better, and the devil take him if he didn't do just that. His shame fueled his determination to not squander this opportunity. He would use this promotion to make a difference, to enact change.

He would show Emilia she wasn't wrong about him.

On the day of the dinner party, Gavin was in the drawing room, morosely ruminating on all of this—how he would handle the evening, how he would make it up to Emilia—when Cora found him. It was midafternoon, but the oil lamps had already been lit. Through the window, the pewter clouds pressed heavily over the woods.

"There you are." She smiled in greeting. "I feel as though I've hardly seen you this week. It always seems to happen during the holidays, doesn't it? All this time together, and yet…"

"I appreciate you inviting me, Cora," Gavin said with a small half smile. "It's been nice to be here, even if I've been more… distracted than usual."

In more ways than one.

"Of course." She squeezed his shoulder. "We're always happy when you visit, even if you need to spend some time on your own. But I'm glad I found you. I wanted to inform you everything is arranged for this evening."

"Ah, about that…" Gavin shifted uncomfortably. He hated to be rude, but…"The children?"

Cora laughed. "Fear not. They won't be at dinner. I'm not so unconventional as that. It will just be Nate and me, you, and our guests. And Miss Davis, as well."

"She's still going to attend?" Gavin asked uneasily.

"She told me she would. Did she tell you otherwise?"

"Not exactly," he muttered.

"Gavin." Cora lifted her chin. For such a small person, she had a great talent for looking imperious. "Is there a reason Miss Davis wouldn't be attending our dinner party this evening? And that she would be discussing it with you?"

"Ah." Gavin sighed. "She's not very happy about the reason for this dinner."

Cora looked at him suspiciously.

"Emilia is upset because I made a mistake. Or rather, I'm in the midst of making one," Gavin admitted. "I thought I was doing it for the right reasons. *Shite.* I don't understand how I've made such a mess of things."

"For the time being, I'm going to sidestep half of the concerning parts of that sentence." Cora lowered herself to the chair beside him. "But, Gavin, you can always talk to me if something is afflicting you. You know that, don't you?"

He was quiet. Faint commotion floated from outdoors. Through the frosty window, Gavin spied Bonnet the mastiff joyfully bounding through the snow; Tess and Leo were bundled up on the terrace, throwing sticks for her. For a moment, he watched them play. Finally, he turned to his sister.

Emilia's words came to him, *one is enough.* But Gavin hadn't helped the one that mattered.

"Cora…I want to apologize."

She blinked in surprise. "What?"

"I did you a great disservice. It's been on my mind, as of late."

"I don't understand." Cora looked puzzled. "You've never done me a disservice, Gavin."

"I did." He fiddled with his spectacles. "With your custody petition. It took me far too long. You were far too close to losing them. I couldn't find a way forward. I couldn't come up with a solution." He drew a painful breath. "I'm sorry…about all of it. And I needed to tell you."

"Gavin." She reached for him. "Why on earth are you sorry? You didn't do anything."

"Exactly." He shook his head. "I didn't do *anything.* If it weren't for Nate…God, I was failing. For months, I failed. I should have been doing more—"

"You weren't failing." Cora sounded distressed. "You held me together that year."

He stared out the window, watching his nephew and niece.

"Gavin…" Cora faltered. "Have you been feeling, this whole time, like you didn't do enough? *You* set everything in motion.

Your plan is what brought Nate to me. It doesn't matter what happened in the end. It was both of you. It was all of us."

He quietly regarded his younger sister, who had lived two lives already. "You *are* happy now, Cora? I believe you are, but you would tell me if you weren't?"

"I am." Her eyes glittered. "I'm so very happy, Gavin. *Unreasonably* happy. So much so, it nearly frightens me if I think about it too much. But Nate..." She broke off. "Every day, Nate reminds me there doesn't need to be a reason. I can trust it."

"Good," he muttered. He thought of Emilia. He wanted to bring her this same contented assurance. *So very happy.* As if it were a given. So freely given, it could make up for all it cost to get there.

"You know..." Cora considered him. "I'm thinking now of when we were children. That festival we attended in Wiltshire. Do you remember it?"

"Ah..." Gavin squinted. "Yes. A bit, I think."

"Our brothers ran off, so it was just me and you, and we each had a farthing. You bought me an apple." She smiled, and Gavin smiled too. "Mother told you not to let go of me, and you didn't. I can still remember eating an apple in the shade of a tree, your hand in mine. No matter how I protested, you would not let go in the crowd."

"There was a juggler," Gavin mused, the memory coming back to him.

"There was. I couldn't look away. I think it was my first enchantment." Cora laughed. "But I asked you—goodness, it's so clear to me—*how does he manage it all? How does he keep all the colored balls aloft?*" She paused. "Do you remember what you told me?"

Gavin shook his head.

"You said it's because he has no choice but to manage it. His entire life is about not dropping a single ball."

They looked at each other, brother and sister, and Gavin took her hand.

"I don't know what struggles you hide from me, Gavin," Cora whispered. "But if I've learned anything in the last two years, it's that it's all right to drop a ball. You never know who might step up to catch it."

She squeezed his fingers, and Gavin finally let go of her hand.

Cora took her leave, but Gavin stayed behind, staring out the window for a long time. Eventually, he roused himself and checked his pocket watch.

He needed to ready for dinner.

For the first time since she arrived at Aldworth Park, Emilia felt uncomfortable.

This was a formal dinner party, not the relaxed and boisterous family meals she'd enjoyed over the last ten days. She had no fancy gown for the occasion, but her dark blue muslin was the nicer of her two ensembles. She affixed her mother's pin in her hair, and, at the last moment, tied her new blue ribbon as a sash. It looked pretty, the light lace against the dark fabric.

In her humble estimation, Emilia thought she looked nice. The blue suited her. Her hair was clean and well-dressed—she'd always been good at that.

But she worried it wasn't enough. Mrs. Travers and Mrs. Norwood would surely be in much finer attire. It would be obvious she didn't fit in. Though knowing what she did about the Norwoods and their opinions of governesses, she wasn't sure she *wanted* to fit in.

She snuffed the candle on her bedside table and went to the corridor, where she found Gavin waiting outside her door. In the flickering light from the wall sconces, he looked painfully hand-some in his evening wear. She newly appreciated that Gavin was a baron's son; he might have to earn his living, but he came from wealth and status. He could attend a formal dinner party on a moment's notice. He would be at ease with the silverware, the removes, the complicated arrangement of courses and dishes.

She nervously touched her hair.

"I thought the loveliest you would ever look was that first night, across the bonfire in the courtyard, when I waited for you to swing back to me during the reel," he murmured with his sweet half smile. "I maintain I was correct. In my mind, you will never look so lovely as that."

"So this is merely the second most lovely?" She softened despite her ill feelings about this dinner.

He shook his head, taking her hand to draw her to him. He put his mouth very close to her ear. "Second most lovely is you bare in my bed, with your hair spilling over the edge and your legs—"

"Gavin!" She flushed from head to boot, her stomach suddenly hot…and many more places besides.

He laughed, low in his throat, and kissed her. She deepened the kiss, opening her mouth to him, easing him against the wall. He hummed, and she felt the vibration in her chest. Her fingers itched for his hair; she wanted to muss him, to bring him into her room, where his fine clothes would be appreciated by nothing but her floor.

She wanted to stay up here with him. Above it.

Finally, she pulled away.

"*This* is the third most lovely," he finished quietly. "All the more so because I know you don't want to do it."

Emilia regarded him somberly. Gavin was on the cusp of his future. He was going to get an important promotion and have an important career, and she wanted to be there with him. Not because of the importance or the promotion, but because of *him*. There was purpose in Gavin; so too was there purpose in loving him. Emilia once thought she was her own best company, but it wasn't entirely true. She was also Gavin's best company. She saw the way she steadied him, the way she drew him out.

She knew how to make this good man better.

She sighed, newly resolved. "Shall we get on with it? At the very least, the food smells divine."

"Always making the best of it." He smiled regretfully.

"Yes, well." She raised her eyebrow, mostly because she knew he couldn't. "One of us has to."

Emilia hadn't liked Bartholomew Norwood on principle, and she didn't like him in person, either. She'd taken his measure immediately, and nothing she'd learned since swayed her opinion. Emilia hadn't only collected whimsical little daydreams from her previous households, she had collected a profound understanding of people.

By now, she had learned some men viewed the world as existing around them.

And some men viewed the world as existing beneath them.

Bartholomew Norwood was barrel-chested and silver-haired and had an oily way about him that left a bad taste in her mouth. Emilia silently watched as he interrupted his wife, swigged his wine, and was the first to laugh at his own snide jokes. He was exactly the sort of person who would leave a mess for others to clean up.

Just as he expected of Gavin.

Emilia concentrated on her soup. She had determined to serve her purpose tonight—to even Mrs. Travers's table, to steady Gavin's nerves—but she would participate no more than necessary. Fortunately, the Traverses were carrying the conversation; Mrs. Travers was unfailingly gracious and Mr. Travers unfailingly charming. Emilia was grateful she didn't have to say much. She suspected Gavin felt the same. Across the table, his knuckles were white around his spoon.

Unfortunately, Norwood had likewise noted Gavin's silence. "I see you're as quiet here as you are at the Inns of Court. Still waters run deep and what not, eh, Sinclair?"

Emilia wrinkled her nose.

"Sinclair is your colleague?" Mr. Travers watched Norwood closely. "Do you keep chambers together?"

"Norwood is a serjeant," Gavin said tightly. "He pleads in the higher courts."

"Soon we'll be colleagues," Norwood interjected. "If he keeps apace, I wager Sinclair will be called to the coif this winter. Will be a nice change, won't it? To have a respite from the racket of criminal trial?"

"I never understood why any barrister would *want* to plead at the Old Bailey." Mrs. Norwood shuddered.

"I don't mind it," Gavin started. "It's really—"

"Man's got to start somewhere," Norwood interrupted pompously, leaning back in his chair. "The criminal courts are a damn good place for a junior to cut his teeth. Sinclair's cross-examination is superb, if you can believe it, what with him acting silent as the grave." He laughed, and Gavin's jaw clicked loud enough for Emilia to hear. "But I presume you're looking forward to more…choice briefs."

"Yes." Mrs. Norwood nodded primly. "Not so many common criminals."

Everyone stared at her.

"Ah…" Gavin frowned. "My duty is to do right by my client." He looked at Norwood. "As to their guilt or innocence, that's for a jury to decide."

Norwood eyed him, his face slowly staining with an unpleasant flush.

The table fell quiet. Mr. Travers stared between Norwood and Gavin.

"Do you have children, Mrs. Norwood?" Mrs. Travers attempted to change the subject.

"We have three," Mrs. Norwood replied. "Our son Samuel was

at Cambridge…" She faltered. "But he's decided to take a little break this term. And our twin daughters are seventeen."

"Oh, I hadn't realized they were grown." Mrs. Travers looked at Gavin. "I would have invited them to join us."

The Norwoods exchanged a glance.

"That was by design, Cora," Gavin said softly. "It would be improper for me to dine with Samuel Norwood."

"Sinclair is my son's defense counsel," Norwood said, holding up his goblet for a refill. "They can only communicate through our solicitor." He smiled disingenuously. "Have to keep up appearances."

"Ah." Mr. Travers tilted his head. "Is that what you're doing?"

"Now, now." Mrs. Norwood forced a laugh. "Let's not talk about unpleasantness at the dinner table—"

"It's no matter," her husband cut in. "It's not a secret Sinclair will plead for Sam." He looked at Mr. and Mrs. Travers. "My son got himself into a spot of trouble with our former governess." He slugged back more wine. "She got too high in the instep, reaching for things beyond her grasp."

Mrs. Travers shifted uncomfortably.

"Fear not." Norwood winked, and it had the opposite effect as when Mr. Travers did it. "Sinclair will put it to rights."

Gavin's jaw popped again, and Emilia spiked with anger. *Shameful.* This man had fewer ethics than Tess when she was angling for biscuits. Not only was Norwood dangling Gavin's promotion over his head, he was flagrantly doing so. Emilia set down her spoon with a clatter.

"It's as I said." Norwood stared hard at Gavin. "Your docket will look quite different come spring, if my recommendation holds." He cleared his throat significantly. "In fact, I prepared a letter, just this morning, to the Chief Justice of the Common Pleas."

Gavin's shoulders tensed.

Mrs. Norwood seemed to find this conversation as dreary as

Emilia found it despicable, for she now turned to Emilia. "Where are you visiting from, Miss Davis?"

All attention swiveled to Emilia.

She had already planned for this. She'd decided to answer these sorts of questions in a very abstract way—she had traveled from Oxfordshire, or perhaps more aptly, Maidenhead. But before she could reply to the inquiry, Bartholomew Norwood dropped his napkin.

It fell to the floor, just at his feet. It was right there; he could easily shift and pick it up. It could have been done already.

But Norwood just looked at the napkin, then deliberately lifted his head and looked at the footman.

And the footman crossed the room, picked it up, and handed it to him.

"Miss Davis?" Mrs. Travers prompted kindly.

Emilia was no longer paying attention. She looked at Norwood's napkin, and then she looked at Gavin. Her heart thundered as she held his dark blue gaze.

Gavin Sinclair was *not* going to pick up after another man. Not if she could help it. Emilia wasn't used to making demands of others, but blast if she couldn't make demands of herself.

At that moment, she understood she was about to do something very, very unwise.

"Oh, I'm not visiting," she finally said. "I work here." She dabbed her mouth lightly and turned to Norwood, her expression sharp. "I'm the governess."

A long silence stretched over the table. Norwood's mouth gaped in a garish smirk of amusement. He looked around, as if everyone were in on a joke.

"Pardon? What did this young lady just say?"

Emilia's voice wasn't quite as steady as she would like it to be. "I'm the governess," she repeated quietly. "So I suppose it's a good thing, after all, your son isn't here."

Norwood's fork dropped with a clatter. His wife gasped.

Gavin coughed and set his spoon down, but Emilia couldn't look at him. She had wanted to shake this repugnant man's facade, but she sensed she'd rattled the wrong person. Gavin asked her to simply make it through this dinner, and a fortnight ago, she would have done just that. The old Emilia, who accepted whatever scraps life gave her, would have eaten her soup in earnest silence.

But Gavin had told her to ask for what she wanted. And what Emilia wanted right now was for him to understand that the Norwood family did not deserve his time nor his good intentions.

"Bold of you, Travers, to invite a hireling to your dinner table," Norwood said slowly.

Emilia closed her burning eyes. She felt woozy and ashamed. *Why* had she said she was the governess?

"Excuse me?" Mr. Travers glowered at Norwood. He was no longer unfailingly charming.

"In my family's experience, you want to watch who you bring under your roof." Norwood lifted his fork, idly dragging roast pork through a sauce Robert. "Just ask my son how quickly a lovely woman becomes an expensive nuisance."

Mr. Travers moved to stand, but Gavin stopped him. "Travers, if I may." He looked to his brother-in-law, who nodded tightly. Gavin pivoted to Norwood; his voice was hard. "Now listen, Norwood—"

"It's fortunate you have no unattached men around here." Norwood laughed humorlessly, his eyes on Emilia. "Except Sinclair."

"If you'll excuse me." Emilia abruptly pushed back her chair. Her bravado had retreated as quickly as it had come on. She needed to leave this dining room. Mrs. Travers reached for her hand, but Emilia was already standing, already withdrawing.

Behind her, there was a sudden, tremendous thud. Out of the corner of her eye, she saw Gavin on his feet. He had thrust back his chair with enough force to knock it over.

"I'm not unattached."

Emilia froze. Tears blurred her vision as she looked at him. Gavin had both hands flat on the table. His ears were red but his jaw was set.

Everyone stared at him.

Gavin Sinclair was creating a disturbance.

"Pardon?" Norwood cocked his head.

"I am not unattached," Gavin repeated. He turned his focus to Emilia, his gaze tender and blazing. "Emilia is going to be my wife."

Everyone spoke at once.

"The *governess*?"

"What? Oh, Gavin!"

"*There* we are. Good man, Sinclair."

"This must be some kind of asinine joke," Norwood barked, his voice laced with disgust. "You're not so foolish as this—to toss aside your prospects—"

Emilia couldn't take in another word. She handled this so badly —the right reasons and a terrible execution. *Oh God.* Gavin's profession. His *livelihood.* She wished with all her heart she could transport herself back to the inn, where a spilled beer was the extent of damage she could cause him. She was always making a mess of things.

She fumbled her way to the corridor, away from the voices in the dining room, her vision blurry and her chest heavy.

You're careless. Because nobody ever cared for you.

Gavin didn't understand. Emilia wasn't careless.

Her life would be so much easier if she were.

15

———————

THE REASON GAVIN SINCLAIR hadn't lost a jury trial in four months was because he was a damn good barrister.

He sometimes forgot that.

But now, with chaos ringing in his ears, Emilia slinking out of the dining room, and Norwood appraising him with that supercilious expression on his stupid bloody face, Gavin remembered.

In a court of law, he never looked at the judge. He never looked at the opposing counsel.

No. All of Gavin's focus went to the jury. Granted, it was markedly easier when he was prosecuting, seeing as a defense counselor wasn't permitted to address the jury in remarks. Finding ways to do so took creativity. He had to rely on his questioning, on his cross-examination.

He relished the challenge; it got him out of his head. Jury trials tended to be brief, as a general rule, but Gavin never rushed. He took his time explaining salient points of law. He was calm. He was thorough.

He liked when he could humanize a difficult concept. He liked when he brought a room of strangers around to his point of view.

And Emilia was right. She was perfectly, patiently *right* about all of it.

And she perfectly, patiently waited for him to catch up to her.

Gavin didn't want to appeal to a jury on behalf of Samuel Norwood, and he couldn't, in good conscience, bring a jury around to his point of view.

Because Gavin's point of view was that the Norwood family was scum.

He was still standing in front of his upended chair. Everyone was looking at him. Everyone, that is, except Emilia, who was the only person who mattered. Gavin presumed she was upstairs; he needed to go there as quickly as possible.

Just as soon as he cleared up this mess, once and for all. Gavin couldn't abide mess.

"Gavin," Cora said slowly. "What do you mean, Emilia is going to be your *wife*? Are you *betrothed* to Miss Davis?"

"I am," Gavin confirmed. Then he paused, mentally combing through his conversations with Emilia. "A bit. I would say at this juncture, betrothal is implied."

Cora made a small sound and covered her face. Nate put a calming hand on her shoulder and eyed Gavin. "Sinclair?"

"I'll see to it," Gavin assured them.

"Surely you jest," Norwood said, narrowing his eyes.

"Almost never, if I can help it."

"I don't understand. " Mrs. Norwood appeared puzzled. "Is Samuel's counsel engaged to a *governess*? I can't imagine the papers will take well to that. The scandal has already been completely blown out of proportion—"

"No," Norwood snapped at his wife. "His counsel is most assuredly not. And we're keeping the damn papers out of it."

"Does your solicitor know that?" Gavin crossed his arms. "It's hard to believe he has time for much besides pandering to *The Times* and courting favor at the junior bar on behalf of your pathetic family."

"Gavin," Cora whispered. She appeared faintly proud and

decidedly appalled. Nate, however, looked as though Christmas had come twice this year.

"You're a smart man, Sinclair." Norwood glowered. "Be smart about this. Your personal affairs could be a conflict of interest—"

"It's not a conflict of interest." Gavin raised his voice a fraction louder than usual, and he was gratified to see Nate, Cora, and the Norwoods fall silent. "I would actually argue this is an alignment of my interests."

Slowly, he bent to pick up his chair. He pushed it in and looked over the length of Cora's beautifully set table. His heartbeat was steady. His breath was even. All at once, Gavin was subsumed by the same unwavering purpose he usually found in his work.

But this was *so much* better.

"I'm finished waiting for the right doors to open for me. I'm not going to do good at the whim of others. I'm doing it where I can, when I can. I'm starting with the woman upstairs."

He speared Norwood with a heavy stare. "You'll be seeing us again. We aren't going anywhere. In fact, we're only getting started. I suggest you write my intended a note of apology." Gavin smiled grimly, feeling both proud and protective. "She just might be kind enough to forgive you. Unlike me."

Norwood scoffed, deep in his throat. "What about my son's case—"

"Your son proposed marriage to Miss Charity Matthews," Gavin said flatly. "If she truly loved him, there may very well be no recompense for the damage done to her." He squared his shoulders. "But I'm damn well going to try."

That settled, he straightened his coat and moved to the door.

Norwood stood and blocked his path. "What do you presume is going to happen, Sinclair? Do you suppose solicitors will bring you briefs after you've shown yourself to be so fickle as this?"

"I don't know." Gavin paused in the threshold and turned to meet Cora's eyes. "But all I need is one."

"Sinclair—"

"That will be all, Norwood." Nate was standing now too, and Gavin was gratified when Norwood had to look up at him. "We are finished here. You've upset my wife, insulted my brother-in-law, and disparaged both his possible betrothed and governesses in general. Forgive me for not having you stay through dessert."

Gavin was already making for the stairs.

It turned out, there was one sort of upheaval he *could* abide.

In fact, he couldn't live without it.

Emilia could see, from a very far distance, she was acting irrationally. She could see it, but she couldn't stop it.

She threw open the trunk to peer at the contents, sifting through the tidy piles. *Nothing.* She slammed the lid closed and turned to survey the disordered bedchamber. The fire crackled, illuminating the full extent of her lunacy.

But no longer did Emilia care about making herself fit somewhere. *She fit.* She fit next to Gavin, who was in the middle of a beautifully arranged dining room, upending his life for her.

Once again, he was making deranged choices, and once again, she was going to hold him accountable.

She couldn't bear it if he looked down now.

Where is it? She needed to find it before she—

"Emilia."

She whirled to face him, too shaken to feel guilty.

Gavin was shadowed in the doorway of his room, surveying the mess she'd made. "What are you doing?"

"I'm looking for the quill I gave you," she said, pushing her hair off her forehead. "I need to find it."

"I was trying to find *you*." He came into the bedchamber, and only now did she see he was breathing very hard. "I went to your room...you weren't there. I thought..."

"Yes. I was here." She yanked open his bedside chest, and there

—*the quill*. She held it aloft victoriously. "I'm taking this back."

She stared at the quill. It was entirely irrational, but right now she felt certain this pen was a tether. If Gavin couldn't write to her, he couldn't leave her.

"You can't take it back." He frowned, slowly striding into the room, stepping over his upended valise. "We've been over this before. You gave it to me. Now it's mine to keep."

"Well, I don't want you to have it." She pointed the quill at him, all of her aching. "I won't stand back this time and just let my life happen to me. I may have ruined everything, but I don't want you to have a *single* recourse. I don't want you to make some pretext—you need to leave, but you'll write to me…and then you *don't*—"

"Emilia." He reached for her hand. Before she could stop him, he pulled the quill away from her, held it in front of him, and briskly snapped it in half. "There."

She stared at the halves of the quill he was holding in his hand.

"See? We don't need it. I promise you, sweetheart, I will *never* write you a letter."

A potent sense of relief coursed through her. She took the broken quill from him and tossed the pieces aside for good measure. No more gifts born of insecurity. She was only going to give Gavin what she knew would last.

"All right." She breathed shakily. "Good."

Her pulse still staggered unevenly, not quite caught up to the rest of her. She lowered herself to the floor and wrapped her arms around her knees. Gavin sank down beside her. They were shoulder to shoulder, leaning against the foot of his bed.

"So…" She pressed the heel of her hand to her forehead. "What happened in the dining room? After I left." She winced, thinking of the catastrophe. "What will happen now?"

"What will happen now," Gavin said forcefully, "is Norwood will eat rot."

"No!" Emilia wiped her cheeks. "I meant what will happen to

you? Gavin, I'm worried for you. Your only intent was to help, and my rash actions harmed your prospects. I was naive and ideological and—"

"And *right*." He turned to her and took her face between his hands. "You were absolutely right. I told him I'm through. I'm not taking his son's brief. I don't want to secure a promotion that way. If the other serjeants want to appoint me, I'll have to take the chance that they will do so with one less recommendation. Though I don't know how much weight Norwood's word will hold once I report his unethical behavior."

His dark blue eyes shone in the firelight. "And, Emilia, if my appointment *does* go through, I'm going to represent Miss Matthews."

She inhaled sharply, clutching his hand. This was the most wonderful news she could imagine.

Slowly, Gavin grinned. "And I'm *damn well* going to win."

Now she clutched his hand for a different reason. Gavin acting so serious and cocksure over liberating a poor woman from ruin? Emilia feared she was in imminent danger of swooning.

"But what about your plans? You had it all arranged, the logical order—"

"The logical order can go to hell."

He slowly threaded his hand through her hair and pressed his forehead to hers.

"Do you know what they call the recompense for a breach of promise suit? What it's called when an injured party is awarded a fine in the face of a broken engagement?"

"No," she whispered. She was cradled against him, his hand warm on her nape, his mouth brushing just above hers.

"A heart balm." He sighed. "That's the term. *A heart balm*. Such a lie, isn't it? The notion a heart can be appraised, a future can be bought. Why do men *insist* on imposing order and sense where it isn't meant to be?"

He ducked his head, holding her gaze.

"The night we met...my God, it was just some winter's evening. There was nothing remarkable about the circumstances, except we were both brave enough to seize them. I shouldn't have found you. Not the first time, let alone the second." He touched her face. "Can't you see? Emilia, there is no logic to the way I love you. It's wide and wild...and it terrifies me." His lips hovered just above hers. "But so is it my balm."

She closed her eyes, and he kissed her, deep and slow, just the way she liked, with his hands wound tight in her hair, holding her fast.

"So this is a bit of a predicament." She smiled softly as they finally parted. "And I don't mean only the state of your room."

"Oh, it's assuredly a predicament." Gavin pushed back his hair, laughing helplessly. "My room. My livelihood. *Your* livelihood. I told you we might need to set it all aside...I suppose we did. It may be a bit of a mess for a little while...possibly a long while. Even if I'm called to the coif, I want to refocus the scope of my work, which will mean fewer briefs. Then, of course, we'll need to afford a marriage license, and new lodgings—"

"Shh." She pressed her fingers to his mouth, quieting his concerns.

"Do you know, I've had the most ridiculous fantasy all my life —a little house I've built in my imagination. It's filled with all sorts of objects I'll never own...and don't really care to own. Because do you know what I wish for, above all else?"

She closed her eyes. It was extraordinary, how clearly she could conjure her tiny sanctuary, how much joy her daydreams brought her. Her life had been so small; she had no idea how big it could be.

"What do you wish for?" Gavin kissed her palm. "Above all else?"

"Two pegs on the wall," she whispered. "That's it. Two pegs on the wall, for two coats to hang, the empty sleeves brushing. *That's* what I want. For someone to watch the door, to wait for me to walk through it. For someone to say, *There you are. Look, I saved a spot for your coat. I saved a spot for you.*"

She laughed shakily. Her heart was fit to burst. "That's all I need. To be loved, exactly as I am. To love you as much as I want. To just...*be.*" She lightly pressed her finger to his chin. "To be myself, with you."

"I can give you that." Gavin took her hand, suddenly, sweetly nervous. "I will always give you that."

He paused, gathering himself. He looked just as he had the first night, when his most insurmountable problem was deciding whether to accompany a stranger to a Christmas party.

Her careful man.

She'd hold the door open for as long as he needed.

"Gavin." She stroked his cheek. "Is there a question you would like to ask me?"

"Right." He took a deep breath, then held her hand between his, squeezing tightly. "Would you care to be the wife of the most diligent barrister in London?"

She was already in his lap, pushing him back to the floor.

"Mind you"—he broke off, accepting her fevered kiss—"I was going to ask you anyway. But thank you for your patience."

"I require an ugly green sofa." She beamed, trailing her lips down his neck. "Will that be a problem?"

"You said two pegs on the wall..." He groaned, wrapping her hair in his fist, drawing her face back to his. He pulled her down for a searing kiss. "You said *nothing* about a sofa."

She laughed, her whole stomach shaking against his.

"You are certain, Emilia?" Another heated kiss, and she was melting above him, her hair unpinned, falling over her shoulder. "It's going to be different for us out there."

She laced their fingers together and gazed down at him. "The view from up here isn't so bad."

He smiled, wide and unfettered.

"No, it's not."

EPILOGUE

DECEMBER 1822

"WE DON'T HAVE time for this," Emilia murmured, even as she slid her palms beneath his braces and backed him to the sofa.

"I assure you, we do." Gavin worked his mouth down her throat. Emilia groaned and tugged his cravat.

"They're supposed to be here in a quarter hour…"

Why she was arguing, Emilia had no idea. She was halfway to pieces already. It had been this way for the last week. Her ardor was becoming rather unwieldy, but Gavin, as ever, was nothing if not a man who would see a job well-done.

"Then we have a quarter hour." His tongue dipped beneath her bodice. "That's time enough for me." He grinned wickedly, already opening his falls. "You're the one slowing us down, my love."

Emilia wasn't sure what was more compelling—the scorching path of his mouth or the fact that her habitually punctual husband was willing to throw aside the clock. He lay back and pulled her over him, sliding her skirts up. Emilia braced her hands on the back of the sofa, the lime green velvet soft beneath her palms. Gavin's fingers trailed higher, teasing her thighs.

"What if they arrive early?" Her question dissolved into a moan at the featherlight pressure of his hand. She dragged her fingers to his hair, furrowing through the thick strands, fisting his curls.

He gazed up at her, his dark blue eyes dilating, navy bleeding to black as he slotted his cock against her aching sex.

"So should I…not?"

"All right, fine, yes," she said, moving against him. "We have time."

In one fluid motion he tugged her hips back, roughly thrusting into her.

"God…*yes.*" She arched her back, holding her skirts around her waist and squeezing her thighs around him the way he liked. She glanced at the clock on the mantel. "Ten minutes, Gavin."

"Relax, sweetheart." He opened the side of her bodice, untying the ribbon on her chemise and yanking it down. He groaned, pressing his face to her breasts and laving her sensitive nipple with his tongue. She hissed, grinding her hips into him. "Ten minutes is plenty."

She closed her eyes as he stroked into her with measured control, pinioning her against him—one hand on her hip, the other beneath her skirts to circle and tease. She tried to give herself over to the sensations, but she couldn't stop looking at the clock; it was *right there,* and now only six minutes—

"Emilia, are you in your head?"

She opened her eyes, glassy and frustrated. "I am," she panted, hitching on a whine. "I'm trying, but—"

"Tell me how you feel." He strummed her clitoris, and her breath snagged. Her fingernails dug into his shoulders, creasing his starched white shirt. "Or…I can tell you how you feel?"

"Yes." She rolled her hips. "That. I think I need—"

"Hot. Wet." He circled harder. "So goddamn *perfect.*" His other hand now kneaded her bottom. "I wish I didn't know. I'll be half-mad the entire afternoon."

He rocked her faster over his cock and Emilia gasped. She looked toward the mantel. *Four minutes.*

"Stay with me." Gavin pinched her hip. "Don't look at the clock. Think of what I'll do to you, the moment we're alone again. When I don't have to rush. When your skirts won't be in my way. When I can take my time."

"Gavin." She could feel herself tipping, the flush starting deep in her belly. Her throat was stained pink; he traced the color with one finger all the way to her nipple. "Keep talking…"

"I love making you come," he panted. "You make me feel so good, Emilia, when you let me take care of you."

He pulled her down to him, changing the angle, and yes—*yes*…

"Shh, that's right," he murmured against her searching mouth. "It makes you feel good too, yes? We're so *good* together." His fingers stroked faster, his thrusts came harder. She was tightening around him, clenching at the pressure. "Show me how good. Come on, Emilia. *Come*—"

She shattered, her hips fused to his, and with two more thrusts, he was there, holding her against him as they both came down. For one blissful minute, they stayed like that, sprawled and still.

"I love you," she breathed, craning her neck.

He smiled at her, lazy and satisfied.

The clock chimed three.

"Good heavens!"

"*Shite.*"

Emilia was immediately on her feet, tugging him to stand, accepting his handkerchief in an attempt to tidy herself. Gavin swore, fumbling his cravat as she hastened to the mirror to fix her hair. She raced to the pitcher in the corner, dipping the handker-chief, wiping her hands before tossing it to Gavin.

"Hurry…hurry—"

A commotion came from outside, followed by a loud series of small, pummeling fists.

"Uncle Gavin!"

"Just a moment," Emilia called, twisting her bodice. She'd

missed a hook. Gavin found it, his nimble fingers refastening her gown.

"Are we ready for this?" He tried to lift an eyebrow, and Emilia smiled. He was getting a little better.

"We're ready."

He opened the door to his new, much humbler, much happier barrister's chambers, and in spilled the Travers children in a loud, chaotic jumble.

"There it is!" Tess barreled through the door, her gaze glued to the sofa. "It's green…it's awful, it really *is*. Mama, look, just like she wrote us—"

The five-year-old catapulted herself to the hideous sofa, and Emilia winced, viscerally recalling what had just transpired in that very spot. She hastily sat down on the offending cushion. Gavin coughed.

"It *is* an awful color, isn't it?" Emilia beamed at Tess. "I adore it."

"Me too." Tess crunched a peppermint, safe at the opposite end of the sofa.

"Me too," Oliver echoed. He upended a basket and turned to Emilia in delight. In the months since she'd last seen him, his chubby cheeks had receded enough to reveal he'd inherited his father's dimples. "What's this?"

"No sweets on Aunt Emilia's sofa," Cora said as she followed the children into the room. "Oliver Travers! What did we say about touching things if we don't know what they are?"

"Not to do it," Leo said severely. He sat at Gavin's desk, point-edly *not* touching the little brass scales.

"How is Ollie to *know* whether he knows what it is if he doesn't touch it?" Tess lifted her chin.

"This one, right here, is the next barrister." Emilia laughed. "Are you so very worried, Nate?"

Her brother-in-law had finally made his way into Gavin's chambers after the rest of his family. "Every damn minute of my life." He grinned, shaking his head. "She's aging me. I found a gray hair yesterday."

"You're thirty-one," Cora pointed out, kissing his cheek. "But yes, it's inevitable with that one."

"Merry Christmas, Emilia." Nate lifted Oliver onto his shoulders. "Are you well?"

"Yes, how are you feeling?" Cora perched next to her. "Is your stomach still upset? Mrs. Edmonds packed up a dozen jars of broth —they're at the townhouse. I'll give them to you when you come for dinner tomorrow."

"My stomach has settled." Emilia sighed, her hand automatically falling to the very faint swell of her belly. It was just starting to be visible now. "Thankfully, my appetite has returned."

She glanced at Gavin; his neck was red. Her appetites had returned in more ways than one.

"Is that how they're knotting cravats in London these days, Sinclair?" Nate smirked, perceptive as always. "It suits you."

Emilia couldn't help but smile. Gavin's cravat was sideways, and his hair flopped over his forehead. So unlike the man she'd met a year ago, slouched over his paperwork. It *did* suit him.

"We won't stay long," Cora assured her. "I know you two are very busy. We just wanted to see the new offices while we're in Town."

"Thank you for coming to London for Christmas this year," Gavin said. "It would have been hard for us to travel, between Emilia's condition and my caseload."

"What are all these notches?" Leo crossed the room to where Emilia had tacked a sheet of parchment to the wall beside an assortment of press clippings. He squinted at the papers. "Oh!" He turned around to his parents in surprise. "This one says Miss Matthews."

"Your governess was the first client in my new practice," Gavin said, coming to stand next to Leo. "That article is about the trial I won for her."

"Is Miss Matthews working out well?" Emilia looked at Cora. She still felt irrationally guilty for abandoning her post so quickly last year, but Cora had scooped up Charity Matthews in the new year and hadn't let her go.

"She's wonderful." Cora smiled. "Leo is starting French this year, and Tess is reading now too."

"Most importantly," Gavin interjected. "She lasted more than ten days."

"So…" Leo ran a finger down the tallies Emilia kept on the wall, then looked at his uncle. "All of these are cases?"

"Yes." Emilia joined them, squeezing Gavin's arm.

"The names are nearly all ladies."

"Yes," Gavin said, looking at the list with Leo. "They are."

Emilia glanced at Cora; she was beaming at her brother, her eyes a little misty.

"Why *is* the sofa green?" Tess was still focused on the important issues.

"Because your aunt insisted." Gavin shook his head. "It was the only way she'd agree to work with me."

"Aunt Emilia is your uncle's secretary," Nate explained. "It means she keeps him in order."

"Is Mama *your* secretary?" Tess frowned.

"No." Nate kissed Cora's hand. "I keep her *disordered*."

"It's wonderful," Cora said decisively, looking around. "The new offices are wonderful, the work is wonderful. I'm so happy for you. For both of you."

Emilia looked around too, unable to stem her smile. She loved their office. She loved their home. She loved their *life*.

"I want to play barrister," Leo said, moving back behind the desk. He picked up a quill, spinning it back and forth. "What do I do?"

"Is there a costume?" Tess asked keenly.

"There is," Nate confirmed. "We will not, however, be giving you access to it."

Nate and Cora's brood passed an agreeable and chaotic half hour in Gavin's chambers, staying until Cora noted Emilia's increasing lethargy. With a swift nod to Nate, Cora rounded up the children, then bussed Emilia's cheek, promising a quieter evening when she and Gavin came to dinner.

And then they were once again alone, together.

Emilia bolted the lock with a sigh, turning to find Gavin already behind her, his arms caging her against the door.

"I thought of another name," he murmured, nuzzling her collarbone. "For the baby."

She laughed. "You were able to think in all of that racket?"

"It was a useful distraction from the fact that Oliver de-alphabetized my case notes."

She twined her arms around her husband and drew him close. "All right. What's the name?"

"What would you say to Belle?" His cheeks were gorgeously pink.

"Belle. Like the inn." Emilia thought it over. "It's quite lovely. And appropriate, seeing as we never did manage to put that evening behind us." She smiled. "But you don't know that the baby is a girl, my love."

Gavin shook his head. "I have a sense. Surrounding myself with women is inevitable at this point."

"You poor man," Emilia teased, running her hand down his arms. "I don't suppose you want a do-over?"

"Hmm." Gavin's mouth ghosted over hers. "So very tempting." He kissed her again. "But I'll decline."

"Oh?" She pushed back his hair.

"Assuredly." He held her gaze, and her heart skipped two perfect beats. Dark blue, like the twilight. Dark blue, like the dawn. "We're only looking ahead."

AUTHOR'S NOTE

*"The life of a nursery governess is worse than that of a maid of all work…
Which, think you, is the best position —an ill-treated, badly-paid nursery
governess, or an independent, well-treated parlourmaid ? I really believe
the latter has the best position, and is thought far more of. Let ladies
pause before entering the ranks of governesses, unless highly
accomplished, and turn their attention to what I have said, and trust me
they will be far happier."*

So wrote "Susan Sensible," the pseudonym of a self-identified governess, to the editor of *The Argus* in 1876. In doing so, she inspired Emilia Davis. You see, I like being in the business of happily-ever-afters, and I took Susan's sign-off as personal challenge: *"[T]hey will be far happier."*

As I started drawing out Emilia's character, I found myself inescapably drawn to the notion of a woman wrestling with insurmountable limitations—and insurmountable loneliness. Susan (probably rightfully) lamented her lot in life; so much so, she wrote to warn other women away from intentionally choosing her circumstances. My heart aches for her, but her letter also made me wonder what it would it be like to write a character who experienced these same struggles.

There are many sources to establish the isolating life of a governess. A class apart from servants but far outside the family, these women often kept to themselves and were expected to adhere to strict rules of propriety. I was especially taken with the stories of "nursery" governesses, those who oversaw a child's primary education but were continually forced to move on as their young charges aged into boarding school, advanced tutors, or societal debuts. It was a lonely and tenuous job, and not a profession women would have selected had they other options. As I sat with Emilia, it became clear that in order to exist in a world laced with so much uncertainty, she'd need a hell of a lot of resilience and a healthy imagination. I was incredibly inspired by her…and so was Gavin. It brought me a great deal of joy to give Emilia a happy home of her own.

The breach of promise suit Gavin grapples with is drawn from legal precedent that existed for hundreds of years—the practice was largely phased out by beginning of the twentieth century, but some jurisdictions in the United States still permit variations of this suit, though they are often not actionable. The premise behind a breach of promise is that an *offer* of marriage is a legally enforceable contract, and it was designed to protect betrothed parties from the fallout of a broken engagement, which could ruin finances and reputations. Eventually, the suit was nearly exclusively brought by women, but in earlier centuries, many suits were also brought by men who likewise suffered the economic sting of a broken engagement…especially when his fiancée's promised dowry was yanked from beneath his feet.

For my research, I used a combination of legal sources and nineteenth-century newspapers. One interesting note is that a breach of promise suit was fairly divisive in the social sense. While a suit could assist poorer women by offering financial recourse for their jilted prospects, the upper classes tended to view these cases negatively, and newspapers and commentators could be harsh critics of those who brought these suits. (There was valid reason for suspicion: there are well-documented cases of women who took advantage of the system by feigning attachments and broken engagements to be awarded sums, but these sensationalized cases were likely the minority.)

Moreover, there is evidence that in the nineteenth century, women themselves had mixed opinions on the usefulness of a breach of promise and the associated "heart balm." While it offered protection, it also kept them in a class apart from men, who traditionally held power in both the engagement and the courts. Women like Charity Matthews endured a great deal of scrutiny and public exposure if they chose to advocate for themselves. And there was always the risk they would go to these drastic lengths for no payoff; the plaintiff and defendant weren't permitted to testify, leaving the suits completely in the hands of counsel, who could make or break a case—and reputation. One scholar who reviewed hundreds of eighteenth- and nineteenth-century breach of promise suits found evidence that some barristers specialized in these cases. I like to think Gavin Sinclair ended up being one of them.

In terms of the trajectory of Gavin's legal career, I had him up for promotion to Serjeant-at-Law, the elite class of barristers who were permitted to plead in the higher courts and, for many centuries, the only barristers who could be named justices in the Court of Common Pleas. By the middle of the nineteenth century, the order of serjeants was declining in favor of King's—or Queen's—Counsel. I decided to put Gavin under consideration for serjeant largely because the mechanism for promotion at that time involved current serjeants making recommendations, which seemed ripe for backroom shenanigans. Gavin was likely too young to be ready for promotion, but as we know, he was a very (*very*) hard worker.

There are plenty of online sources that describe late-Regency Christmas traditions; I utilized some well-established customs and tweaked others to fit my characters. Saint Thomas Day was when the elderly and widowed went thomasing for charity, and on Saint Stephen's Day (Boxing Day), servants received donations from their employers. Christmas celebrations occurred from Stir-Up Sunday (the first Sunday of Advent) through Twelfth Night, so while Gavin believed the Belle's Christmas party was unfashionably early, the proprietor and I disagree! A common belief in this period was that it was bad luck to decorate before Christmas Eve, but anyone familiar with Cora Travers would be unsurprised to learn she can't help herself at the holidays (besides, she already had her fair share of bad luck). As for Christmas presents, some sources indicate the most popular days to exchange gifts were the feast of Saint Nicholas or the Epiphany, but other sources describe giving gifts on Christmas Day. I always appreciate that customs will vary by region and by family, and I personally loved creating traditions for Aldworth Park that were *just* to the left of conventional.

REFERENCES

English Miscellanies. (1827, July 24). *The Monitor*, p. 4. https://trove.nla.gov.au/newspaper/article/31758657#

Colonel Berkeley and Miss Foote. (1824, December 23). *The Sun (London)*,p. 3. https://www.britishnewspaperarchive.co.uk/viewer/BL/0002194/18241223/009/0001

Governess or Lady Help? (1876, July 3). *The Argus (Melbourne, Vic.)* p. 6. https://trove.nla.gov.au/newspaper/article/5893790#

Hughes, K. (2014, May 15). *The Figure of the Governess*. The British Library. https://www.bl.uk/romantics-and-victorians/articles/the-figure-of-the-governess

Frost, Ginger Suzanne. "Promises broken: Breach of promise of marriage in England and Wales, 1753-1970." (1991) Diss., Rice University. https://hdl.handle.net/1911/16441.

Roscoe Pound, Legal Profession in England from the End of the Middle Ages to the Nineteenth Century, 19 Notre Dame L. Rev. 315 (1944). Available at: http://scholarship.law.nd.edu/ndlr/vol19/iss4/1

Polden, Patrick, 'Barristers', *The Oxford History of the Laws of England: Volume XI: 1820–1914 English Legal System*, The Oxford History of the Laws of England (Oxford, 2010; online edn, Oxford Academic, 1 May 2010), https://doi.org/10.1093/acprof:oso/9780199258819.003.0031, accessed 21 Sept. 2023.

ACKNOWLEDGMENTS

I'd like to thank the many people who helped shape this novella with their lovely and patient input. To my beta readers: Lindsay Barrett, Amy, and Celine Oliver–thank you for making time and space for this wintry story in the dead heat of summer! Sarah T. Dubb: your excellent eyes, excellent heart, and excellent good humor have been an absolute gift. Thank you for making this process so fulfilling and so damn fun. And to the intrepid denizens of SF2.0: thank you for your excitement and support, and for all of the many titles that I did not end up using. Y'all are the best (and punniest!)

I'd like to especially thank Anjor for remaining the best advocate for my words, and for telling me (time and again) they will come when they come, and for taking such good care of them when they do. I'd like to go on the record that you were Gavin's first fan, and when I was uncertain of his Romantic Hero Allure, you had an arsenal of evidence to prove me wrong. Thank you for standing by your man! (But most of all, thank you for standing by me.)

Many thanks to my cover designer, Erin Dameron-Hill, who once again blew me away. And of course my editor, Rachel Shipp, who has such wonderful talent for bringing my story to life. Thank you for all of your work to propel my vision forward! It's a dream to work with you.

To my readers, especially those who supported my debut novel, *Forever Your Rogue*. You all quite frankly changed the course of my life. Thank you from the very bottom of my heart for embracing Nate and Cora's story and the world of my characters. I'm so grateful, every single day. I hope you think of this as my holiday gift to all of you!

And finally, to my family. I have the most patient husband and children imaginable. Adam, thanks for telling me to write another book (even if you can't read it); Claire, thank you for your input on the "cover lady's" dress. And Pete: thank you for my very favorite love story. Every word I write starts with you.

ABOUT THE AUTHOR

Erin Langston is a historical romance author who crafts Regencies with heart, heat, and humor. A librarian by trade, Erin lives in the Midwest with her husband and two children. When not working, writing, or mom-ing, she can be found outside, drinking wine, buried in a book, or attempting to home-improve. A not-insignificant portion of her first novel was plotted in the preschool pickup line.

erinlangstonwrites.com

ALSO BY ERIN LANGSTON